Moonlight Danger

Hot Moon Rising Book 5

By
Tina Donahue

Copyright © 2016 by Tina Donahue
ISBN: 978-1-68361-035-9
Cover art by Mina Carter

Published by Decadent Publishing Company, LLC
Look for us online at:
www.decadentpublishing.com

~A Note from the Author~

For a long time, I've loved shifter stories and finally wrote my first, *Pleasure Me*, for Decadent's Black Hills Wolves series. I enjoyed the plot so much I knew I had to do more shifters. You can imagine how thrilled I was when Desiree Holt invited me to be one of the launch authors for her scorching new series, Hot Moon Rising.

With Nick and Portia, my lovers in *Moonlight Danger,* I've explored the hazardous world a shifter inhabits, not only from the human but the wolf side. At times, nothing is as it seems. Danger seems to lurk everywhere. However, I also wanted the story to focus on Portia and Nick's romance—uber steamy but with sweet and tender moments. What I like to call heat with heart. My author brand.

Already, the Moonlight pack is a part of me. I can't wait to see where this series goes with the other talented authors bringing this shifter world to life.

I'd love to hear what you think about Nick and Portia's story. You can reach me at: tinadonahuebooks@gmail.com

Dedication

To those lucky couples who've found true love a second time.

Moonlight Wolf Pack

Charlie Aquino (human) – Detective for the sheriff's gang task force for Palmetto County Sheriff's Department. His partner is Jesse Farrell.
- Mate: Liana Cosa

Liana Cosa Aquino – Refugee from a different pack. She works part-time as a waitress at Moonlight Diner.
- Mate: Charlie Aquino

Alexa Martin Farrell – Left her pack over a disagreement with her alpha. She moved to Florida and helped the pack find a small community of cottages in Moonlight, Florida. She works as an Internet researcher and gets jobs through her online website. She also does research for The Defenders.
- Mate: Jesse Farrell

Jesse Farrell (human) – Detective for the sheriff's gang task force for Palmetto County Sheriff's Department. His partner is Charlie Aquino.
- Mate: Alexa Martin (who saved him when on assignment he was attacked by a gang)

Riesa Marlowe (human) – A psychic who helped locate Hannah Raines.
- Mate: Derek Sawyer

Hannah Raines Molina – She was kidnapped and saved by Jesse and Charlie with the help of Riesa Marlowe, a psychic. Works as Alexa Martin's research assistant.
- Mate: Rand Molina

Rand Molina - Derek's second-in-command in the Moonlight pack. Partners with Derek Sawyer at The Defenders, a private security agency.
- Mate: Hannah Raines

Derek Sawyer – Alpha of a small pack, most of their original clan was destroyed when developers took the land they were living on and many of their pack were killed by hunters. They hid in an abandoned orange grove until Alexa offered them the bungalows in exchange for their help. He and the others have embraced Jesse & Alexa and Charlie & Liana and given the female shifters a new sense of belonging.
- Partners with Rand Molina at The Defenders Agency, a private security and bodyguard agency.
- Mate: Riesa Marlowe

The Defenders Agency - A private security and bodyguard agency formed by Rand and Derek once they were established in the little enclave of cottages. It provides good income for the pack. A majority of the pack is involved in the cases they take.

Jesse and Charlie are their contacts with the sheriff's department and also refer many cases to them.

Chapter One

Nick Wyatt stepped into the bungalow kitchen, stopped dead, and should have run. Welded to the spot, he drank in the scene, his mouth going dry.

Portia Danes reclined on the black-and-white linoleum, long legs stretched out, skin sun kissed to a rich caramel color. A dainty rose tattoo graced her right calf, a kid's Band-Aid on her left knee, the strip depicting what looked to be a mermaid. Maybe that had been her fave cartoon character as a kid. She was twenty-six now. Lush. Ripe. Pure female. He lost his smile. Perspiration rolled down his chest, his reaction having nothing to do with the sticky May afternoon. Her heady scent surrounded him—clean skin, a flowery shampoo or soap fragrance, and musk. A woman and she-wolf's provocative aroma.

He leaned against the jamb for support. Leaving still wasn't an option.

Blindly, she groped for a tool to her side, selecting an odd-looking wrench he couldn't identify, since he wasn't a plumber. In his thirty years, he'd never seen one dressed as she was now. Pink socks with lacy edges peeked past the tops of her work boots. Her denim overall-shorts were more Daisy from Dukes of Hazzard than a Future Farmers of America member toiling in the tomato fields. Her tank top was also pink, matching her cute socks.

She worked the tool and grunted, her left heel digging into the floral bedsheet beneath her, creating an oddly provocative scene. Like a woman in the throes of passion, fighting against release, wanting the pleasure to continue for hours with him naked and willing above her.

His senses roared into overdrive. His cock thickened painfully. Time to go. Actually, well past that point. He didn't need her complicating his life. Nor did he deserve happiness or peace—a matter his friends had argued against, telling him every wolf needed a mate.

Easy for them to say. They hadn't gone through what he had.

Portia's tool rattled against the floor. She pulled the pen flashlight from between her lips, scooted out, and gave him a wide, welcoming smile. "Hey."

His mouth refused to work, every word he'd known drifting away. Chestnut tresses cascaded over her shoulders, blonde streaks on each side framing her face. He would have bet his life her hair was softer than kitten fur. The green flecks in her hazel eyes were amazing. Her pouty lips looked moist, the same as they'd be after him kissing her long and deep. His balls ached. "Ah...."

She leaned back, legs drawn up like a 1950s cheesecake drawing. Sweetly sensual. "You're ready to do the floor?"

He gripped his roll of linoleum. "Not until tomorrow."

He'd planned to drop off the material, not run into her. Doggedly, Nick had avoided Portia since she'd joined the pack, hoping out of sight would be out of mind. Yeah, right. Her scent permeated everything, teasing, enticing. Too many nights he'd awakened in a sweat, panting from his wet dreams, followed by remorse over his past sins. He placed the roll near the wall. "Didn't know you'd be here."

Understanding flashed across her pretty face mingled with disappointment. She was on to him. Hell, anyone older than seven would have caught on to how he'd continually dodged her.

He gestured to the sink. "Go on. Don't let me bother you."

"You're not." She smiled softly, making a small dimple.

His legs went watery. The air grew increasingly charged. Longing and lust bombarded him. He stepped back.

"I actually hadn't planned to be here today." She put her wrench into a portable toolbox the Hulk would have had trouble carrying. "Thought I'd fixed this stupid thing days ago." She inclined her head to the sink. "Derek told me it was still leaking like crazy. Not only that, but the garbage disposal cord is frayed. Don't know how I missed something so basic. If water had gotten on it while it'd been running, someone might have been hurt. Electrocuted. It could have caught fire. Good God, they would've died."

"Hey, hey, hey, it didn't and nobody was harmed. No reason to feel bad." Guilt remained his old friend, and he didn't want it hounding her. "You'll fix it, right?"

"The pipe's good, again, or at least I hope it is. The rest will have to wait until morning. It's getting too late to work with the lights off."

Sun streamed through the window, creating long shadows. Dust particles danced in the weakened rays. Soon, it would be dark. She had her flashlight, though, and could also unplug the disposal then turn the main switch back on to light up this place. He probably should have mentioned those alternatives, but didn't, not wanting to sound bossy or too interested in her work.

She packed her things and slanted him a look. "You finished for the day?"

Thankfully. It had been a long one. His construction work on several bungalows should have exhausted him worse than a ten-mile run on two feet rather than four. Oddly, he was too alert. His heart wouldn't stop thudding, shooting so much heat through him his tee clung to his damp chest and back. "Yeah."

Joy lit her features.

He pointed behind himself. "I should be going."

"Me, too. Wait up and we can walk to our places together." Hurriedly, she gathered the bedsheet, stuffing it in her toolbox. After shoving the top down and throwing the clasps, she grabbed the handle.

"Whoa." Nick put out his hand. "How much does that weigh?"

"Less than you. Me too probably."

She couldn't have been more than a hundred-and-twenty pounds soaking wet. Her curves were in all the right places, from her voluptuous rack to her shapely hips. She embodied every straight guy's fantasy and appeared in Nick's dreams most nights. "I'll do the heavy lifting."

"Where were you when I needed someone to carry my purse?"

He laughed. The thing did look like a small suitcase. He'd seen her lugging it on her way out of town, paying too much attention to her when he shouldn't have. His unquenchable interest couldn't lead anywhere, certainly not to mating. That and love weren't in the cards. He wanted a simple, uncomplicated fuck to take off the edge, but wouldn't do that to her. Any other woman—human or shifter—he considered fair game, as long as they knew the score. Not her. Never her. She deserved better than him.

Sobering, he grabbed her toolbox, lifting it higher than necessary. The weight made his shoulders and back scream. His ego said, "Screw it, show off." He didn't want to examine why. "Not heavy at all."

To prove his lie, he swung the box back and forth.

She leaned in. "Careful. Blood vessels are popping in your eyes. Your jugulars will be next."

He pressed his lips together, but his laughter still broke free. "If I didn't know better, I'd say you had a dead body in here."

"Nope. Only my makeup."

"You wear that stuff?"

She gave him an odd look. "I'm not sure whether I should be offended or not."

"Sorry. What I meant to say is you don't need it."

"That's the spirit. I should help you carry that."

He pushed her hand away gently, and their fingers touched for a long moment. Desire jolted through him. Her skin was warmer and silkier than he'd believed possible. Her breath caught as his did. He broke free first and slogged outside, gulping soupy air. A full month from summer and already the temps were oppressive, high eighties, the humidity punishing, the heavy foliage wrapped in a steamy haze. He blinked sweat from his eyes.

She pressed a lacy handkerchief to her forehead and throat then offered it to him.

Nick fought an unbearable urge to lift the snowy linen to his nose to see if it smelled like her. "I shouldn't. I don't want to mess that up."

"You won't."

Laughter bubbled in his throat. Several beach towels and an industrial-strength fan wouldn't have made him less sweaty. He needed to calm down. How though, except to cave to his inner urges concerning her, or change into the beast and run, howling like a banshee or a wolf torn by lust, guilt, regret. Thankfully, no one in the pack was around to see his turmoil. Everyone remained at work or were in their cottages, enjoying a late dinner, TV, video games, wild monkey sex, whatever the hell they did.

"Doing okay?" Portia searched his face.

He figured veins were popping out on his forehead. "Great."

His legs were leaden, and the box pulled down his arm. He plodded toward their bungalows, both set apart from the others. Hers the most, flanked by moss-draped oaks and palms, the perfect lovers' getaway. His pulse sprinted. In the increasing gloom, her cottage looked more rose than pink, the color she'd chosen for it, and possibly the same shade as her nipples and cleft.

Shouldn't think about that. He concentrated on the burning ache in his arm and elbow from carrying the toolbox, finally reached her porch, and glanced right, left. She wasn't beside him.

He hung on to the box, on the outside chance she might need it, and backtracked to where she'd stopped two houses away, her profile to him. A faint pulse beat in her long throat, begging for his mouth and tongue. He kept his distance. "What are you doing?"

She kept sniffing and frowned. "Don't you smell that?"

He didn't bother inhaling. Her fragrance seemed a permanent part of everything surrounding him. "What?"

She strode to the vegetation, nose lifted.

Her thighs were seamless, nothing but tanned, flawless skin.

She pivoted. He glanced up. Her expression said she'd caught him eyeing her. Heat burned his face and scalp. Warmth poured to his groin, settling there, making him too hard, and fucking miserable. "What did you smell?"

"I'm not sure...nothing. Thanks for carrying my stuff. How about I grill some steaks to pay you back for your muscle?"

"No need."

She waved dismissively. "I know that. But it'd make me feel better for causing your bloodshot eyes. Face it, that baby's heavy even for you."

"You think?" Teeth clenched, he hefted the box above his shoulder.

"Careful or you'll give yourself a hernia." She wagged her finger. "Come on. Dinner's the least I can do for you nearly popping an artery."

She jogged to her house, gesturing for him to follow. Her bouncing buttocks pulled him like metal to a magnet. Once he'd put the box inside her front door, he followed her to the backyard, more heavily vegetated than the front. Within a small clearing stood a white bench large enough for two adults or three kids, a battered barbeque grill, and a small sliver of water that ran through her property line, petering out before reaching his.

"Before I cook our steaks, do you mind if I cool off first?" She already sat on the ground, untying and tossing her boots aside. Her adorable socks followed. She'd painted her toenails deep red and had another flower tat on her ankle.

Nick wanted to taste it, his mouth watering.

"Can you believe it's so hot already?" She unhooked her overalls straps and unbuttoned each side of the garment near her hips.

"What?"

"It's hot, don't you think?"

She leaned back, wiggled out of her overalls, and tossed them aside. Her panties were a scrap of some silky material edged in pink lace. He wouldn't have expected any other color. "Ah...."

She dropped her tank top on the denim. Her boobs filled her pink bra near to overflowing, the gentle mounds quivering with each movement and breath. Effortlessly, she glided the straps off her arms, unhooked the bra back, and lobbed the garment onto her growing clothes pile.

He stepped forward without meaning to, transfixed by her nipples, a deep rose as he'd guessed, puckered and tight, ready for a man's mouth.

Portia didn't flaunt her partial nudity. She appeared far more casual than he as she slipped off her panties. No wait, she'd worn a thong. His skin tingled.

She chucked the underwear on top of her bra and stood. "You must be hot, too. Want to join me? Plenty of room."

Nick figured she'd gestured to the water, but he couldn't concentrate on anything except the springy curls between her legs. That delicate pelt was as dark as her other hair. Her cleft and puffy lips pointed the way to paradise. At least for a little while. After that....

He should leave.

She padded to him, taking his hands. "Join me when you're ready. We have all night. I'm not going anywhere but here."

Three small moles circled her navel, fascinating him. A light sprinkling of freckles graced her shoulders. Although tall and athletic, she was surprisingly narrow, seeming so delicate.

She had more courage than he did, facing him with unashamed desire and patience.

Nick wanted to make a move but couldn't quite break free from the past, telling himself he shouldn't. He deserved to remain alone forever. She kissed his knuckles. His lids slipped down. He ached with need and resistance.

True to her word, she stayed relatively close, slipping into the water, the brief waves lapping her thighs. "Wow. Almost as good as a shower."

She poured water over her shoulders, breasts, and belly. Her delicate curls trapped the moisture that sparkled in the remaining daylight. Soon, the heavy moon would rain its silvery light on them. If he were still here, which he wouldn't be.

He edged closer to the bank.

After dampening her neck, she lay on her back, floating, face turned to him.

He didn't recall taking off his work boots, socks, jeans, or tee. When he wore nothing except his stretchy boxer briefs, he considered what he was doing.

She patted the water, encouragingly. "Hop on."

"On?"

"In. Always mix those up. Come on, you need to cool off."

With both of them in there, they'd probably bring the damn stream to a boil. Warning bells rang. Loneliness and lust won. Shutting down his misgivings, Nick peeled off his underwear. He stood above her, naked and fully aroused, letting her get her fill of the man, the beast he was.

***

A pulse ticked deep within Portia's sheath. Nick called to everything female within her.

He was a large man, over six-three, all bronze skin and hard muscle, his abs and pecs superbly defined. Days spent in hard labor, and nights as a prowling wolf, had toned him beyond belief. Dark hairs rounded his navel, trailing down his hard belly to the heavy thatch on his groin. His cock jutted from those fragrant curls, his shaft thick and long, ropey veins snaking down its length, his plump crown the same ruddy shade as his balls. They were tight to his body, lightly furred. One zillion percent male.

She couldn't breathe, swallow, think about anything except him being inside her. Them face-to-face, burrowing into each other's bodies and souls, gazes locked.

He was so beautiful she could have looked at him for years on end. He wore his raven hair shaggy and long, the ends curled around his ears and neck. A stunningly masculine effect further accentuated by his rough good looks. His lushly lashed eyes were black and piercing, the animal within barely contained.

She wanted his wolf side unleashed, uninhibited, primitive. He could be as savage with her as he desired. She wasn't afraid. Nick was a good man.

Too good. He heaped blame on himself for what had happened to Bree. No words would convince him otherwise. Months ago, when Portia had come to the pack as a refugee, she'd had her own sorrow to deal with, hoping only to be with other shifters, never dreaming she'd meet him.

Since that day, she'd hungered for a few words, a smile, touch, embrace. He'd been stingy with his affection and time, always running away. She couldn't blame him, but she couldn't abide their separation any longer. Time to move on from the past into the present, to live and love.

She pushed to her feet and offered her hand.

He laced his fingers with hers, sending a thrilling shock to her core. Struggling for control, she dug her toes deeper in the cool mud.

Nick slipped into the water, his musky scent bearing a trace of leather from his soap or aftershave. Totally virile. Completely irresistible. Once he'd gained firm footing, they were only a breath away.

Might as well have been miles. His gaze cleared suddenly and grew cautious. Before he changed his mind about this, she stroked his bristly cheek and upper lip, adoring the rasp. "Have a hard day?"

His stiffened cock bobbed on the water, the crown stroking her thigh. He nodded.

She edged closer. "How about I massage your shoulders."

"You don't have to— Fuck that's nice."

She worked her fingers into his tense muscles, kneading them with care. "Relax."

His head lolled back, his prominent Adam's apple begging for a kiss, his hair-roughened throat inviting her to mark him with a hickey.

She resisted both impulses. For now. Later, all bets would be off. "I'd tell you to sit down, but I don't want you to wash away."

Chuckling, he slid his feet farther apart.

"Here." She lifted his arm to her waist. "Hold on to me and I'll do the same with you. That way neither of us will fall."

"Or we both will."

Would that be so bad? He was as alone and

wanting as she was. No matter how successfully he'd denied his human side, the wolf in him needed a mate. She inched closer, making certain his cock had nestled against her pussy.

At last, he snuggled his arm around her, his limb heavy and warm, exactly what she craved. She eased his hair off his neck and massaged him even better than before. "Feel good?"

He inhaled deeply, blowing out his breath. "God yeah."

"Were your shoulders aching from carrying my box?"

"No. My eyes were."

She liked his teasing. "Open them. I want to see the damage."

"No, you don't. If I don't close my eyes, they'll fall out."

"Poor baby." She tilted his face to her and kissed his lids.

He stilled.

Leaves rustled to the side. He looked over, avoiding the moment they'd shared, at least emotionally. His rigid shaft pressed against her mound, thicker than before. He might have been able to pretend nothing had happened between them with his neutral expression and silence, but his cock didn't lie.

He loosened his hold on her.

She stroked his pec, enjoying how his muscles jumped. "How about you return the favor and give me a massage? I work hard, too." She eased around, her ass to his groin, his shaft snug against the seam between her cheeks. "Go on. I won't stop you."

He made a noise somewhere between a chuckle and wanting groan. "About you working hard...."

"There won't be any new leaks." For the life of her, she couldn't understand how the pipe could have been so messed up after she'd worked on it. Or how she could have forgotten to replace the frayed cord with the new one she'd bought at Kent's, a lumber–hardware store in Palmetto. She'd been so certain she switched the bad cord with the good one, but hadn't. Sure, she was tense from no sex, affection, and not having Nick pressed close to her like now, but she wasn't a slacker or fool when it came to her work. "I did the job right this time."

"Yeah, about that." Gently, he rubbed her shoulders.

She sagged against him, unable to resist. "About what?"

"Huh?"

He'd pressed his face into her hair, sniffing deeply. Nice.

"Ah, your work." He eased back. "Where'd you learn to fix pipes?"

"You sound surprised. Is that in a good or bad way?"

"Neither. And I'm not. Okay, I am a little. You don't strike me as the usual plumber type."

"Why?"

"Your socks and overalls for one. Then there's the cartoon Band-Aid."

"I cut my knee. Didn't want to bleed to death."

"Did you get your near-fatal injury doing plumbing?"

Shaving her legs this morning. The Little Mermaid Band-Aids were all she could find at the discount drugstore, unless she'd opted for Spider Man. No contest.

"What's wrong with my clothes?" She'd dressed especially for Nick, trying to be hot plus competent. Not easy for a female plumber slash maintenance person. "You don't like what I wear?"

"No. I mean, yeah I do. I mean—" He huffed out a breath and pressed his cheek against hers. "You're a woman. I haven't seen many rummaging around beneath sinks."

She stroked his jaw. "I don't rummage, I repair."

"Right. You took shop? You went to a trade school to learn this? A boyfriend taught you?"

"I actually taught the guys I dated." All three of them. She hadn't been popular in high school or after. Could be because she'd been the only shifter in town with everyone sensing something was strange about her. "I learned what I know from my father. Would have taken over his business if he and Mom hadn't died."

Nick made a pained sound. "Sorry, I didn't mean to bring up anything bad."

"You didn't." She turned into him and cupped his face. "I'm happy we had the time together that we did. They were great people, but I have to move on.

That's why I came here. To be with my own kind." She touched her fingers to his lips before he could speak. "I know you're not looking for anything permanent. That's okay. This can be purely physical. We can have fun. I don't know about you, but I really need that."

His expression changed from surprised, to troubled, to something she couldn't read. "You deserve better."

"I deserve now. Neither of us is going to be around forever. Who knows what tomorrow will bring. Something could happen to me and then I'd never have this chance."

"Don't say that. Never say that."

"Hey, it's okay. I'm trying to be realistic. Why not enjoy the time we're here and have some—"

His kiss stopped her, his tongue plunging deep into her mouth, exactly what she needed. He growled like the wolf he was and cupped her breast, squeezing roughly, his control ended.

He tasted exquisitely clean, his unique flavor proving his youth and health. She pressed closer, wanting him more than air or food, his heat and size intoxicating. Water sloshed around their legs. They grasped each other harder and tottered, trying to remain upright.

He pulled free and sucked air. "Let's go."

She held back. "Where?"

"The bank." He pointed. "To lie down."

"My bed's inside the cottage."

"Too far."

Best answer ever.

He helped her to ground level and spread their clothes as a makeshift sheet. From here on out, she'd make certain there was always one out here at the ready.

Joined in a new kiss, they sank to the ground and rolled right, left, both trying to get on top. He won. Awesome.

With one hand, he held her wrists above her head and swooped down, suckling her neck.

Her pussy creamed. Deluged with pent-up desire, she gave into animal heat, wrapping her legs around his lean hips, pushing her fingers through his wonderfully thick hair. He laved her nipple, making the tip harder, his suckles freeing her basest core. She ached for him to fuck her until they were both raw then start over, not stopping for weeks, months, maybe ever.

She was losing it and couldn't have been happier.

On a lusty grunt, he edged down, licking her navel, making her laugh. He gave her furry mound his most ardent attention, burying his nose in her curls, smelling her excitement. Their musk filled the air, the scent heavy, decadent, promising.

With his hands beneath her buttocks, he feasted on her puffy folds. She bucked and pushed into him, giving herself fully. She'd lied when she'd said this was solely about sex. He already burned in her blood and marrow. She'd known that when their gazes first met at a pack meeting called by Derek, the head honcho here. He'd asked everyone to speak up on whether to accept her or not.

Nick had been the first to approve, unable to look away from her, the same as she'd been with him, hearts opening to each other, futures endless if only he'd allow himself more than tonight.

Right now was all she had and wouldn't waste a precious moment. She clutched the clothes beneath her and wrapped her legs around his neck, hanging on, needing an anchor against the mounting tension in her cunt. He licked and suckled her clit. Nerve endings fired wildly, electrifying her nub. Heat shot from her thighs to her belly, lingering then building. She thrashed her head from side to side, fearing she wouldn't last. She hadn't experienced pleasure in too long, a man wanting, cherishing, loving her always out of reach.

Until him.

He might have only desired her now, but that was a good start.

She gritted her teeth and arched her back to fight off orgasm, wanting to savor this slice of time, needing it to last. A carnal storm raged within, unstoppable and overwhelming. Someone shouted. Might have been her, she didn't know. Too much bliss crashed through her, snatching what breath she had, ringing her ears, leaving her weaker than a newborn.

Panting, she let her legs flop down, gripped his hair, and reeled him in, claiming his mouth. Being apart from him wasn't an option. He had to fill her in some way at all times. They kissed noisily, artlessly. Form didn't matter, satisfaction did. She pressed so hard into him, his teeth dug into her bottom lip. No biggie. This was worth the pain.

He finally broke free, hair hanging over his forehead, his expression damn near barbaric.

She gripped his biceps. "Fuck me."

He plunged inside, driving his meaty cock deep within her sheath, not stopping until their curls touched and he'd stretched her farther than she believed possible. They clung to each other, her kissing his neck, him suckling her shoulder and flexing his rod. Showing off as he had when he'd lifted her two-ton box.

Delighted, she tightened her cunt around his cock, prepared to give him a ride he'd never forget. He eased back, looking dazed, though not enough to keep him from pumping. Each thrust was forceful and precise, his withdrawal from her timed to when she squeezed her pussy around his shaft, increasing the friction between them.

A familiar and pleasant ache coiled within her mound. She dug her fingers into his arms, braced for release. Relief arrived from nowhere and all sides, surprising and powerful, euphoria sweeping through her, making her insatiable, hungering for more.

He came next, bellowing like the animal he was, perspiration running down his face and chest, arms trembling.

Portia guided him to her chest, comforting and protecting him at his most vulnerable. Not that she didn't have a little sass left, too. She worked her hand between them and stroked his balls.

He shuddered. "Shit, don't."

"Sorry." She squeezed her pussy around his rod.

"God. Stop."

She did for the moment. "There's no pleasing you, is there?"

He laughed tiredly. "It's too much. Give me a sec."

She'd give him a lifetime. All he had to do was ask. "Sure."

She embraced him, relishing their mingled scents. Her smelling of him, him smelling of her.

The mild breeze picked up, an odor intruding. This one frightening, disturbing. The same stench as before when she'd asked if he'd smelled it, too. Odd that he hadn't then or didn't seem to now. She'd only encountered it once in her life, hoping never again to face that unmistakable smell.

Death.

Chapter Two

Portia stiffened beneath Nick. With stunning speed, he snapped out of his sex-induced fog and pushed to his elbows. "I'm too heavy. Are you all right?"

"I'm fine." She cupped his shoulders to ease him back down. "You're not too heavy. You're perfect."

That assessment was so far from the truth, he should have roared with laughter. Perfect would have been him enjoying her mindlessly, then leaving without a backward glance. He wasn't anywhere close to that truth. Her loving caress warmed and comforted. Having his cock burrowed deep within her gave him a taste of everything he'd missed, wanted, and feared. To have her once more or even a million times would never be enough. He'd crave her ceaselessly, guilt eating him alive, destroying her, too. She should have listened when he said she deserved better. He shouldn't have been such a goddamn horny prick to forget that.

He pulled out of her and tugged his jeans from beneath her leg.

She cuffed his wrist as well as she could. "What are you doing?"

"I have to go."

"Why? We've barely started. We haven't eaten. You can snooze while I grill the steaks. Or, if you're hardcore about it, you can handle the meat like men think they're supposed to. No judgment here."

He wanted to laugh and love her clear until tomorrow. After prying her hand away, he kissed her knuckles. "I need to leave. Sorry."

As he gathered his things, he couldn't look at her. Her sighs were already tearing him apart. He clutched his clothes to his chest and padded naked across her brief yard into the heavy vegetation that led away from her house and his. Going home to lose himself in sleep was out of the question. He needed to flee physically. If he'd been a bird, he would have taken flight, soaring above the earth until nothing on it was recognizable.

Portia's face swam before him, the details too acute. Her eyes sparkling with desire in the pearly light, lids slipping down with her release. Her dimpled smile relaxed with satisfaction, breasts quivering with his every thrust. The easy slide of his rod within her pussy, his shaft damp from her juices.

A primal urge to mate nearly knocked him down. He strode faster then jogged through the dense foliage. Twigs and rocks bit into his soles. Saw palmettos whipped his calves and thighs. The discomfort energized Nick. Around him, the forest came alive, sounds pressing in. Vegetation rustling from animals trying to escape notice. A motor in the distance, the engine coughing, trying to die. Water gurgling over rocks. His hammering heart.

He released his clothing and stilled, the change inevitable now, each cell within him screaming for freedom from his human form, the man he no longer wanted to be. His fingers trembled then his hands and arms until he quivered violently, similar to a flag in a stiff breeze. He experienced no physical pain, only boundless liberation, embracing his inner beast, skin roughening with short, black hairs, nose and teeth elongating, limbs morphing.

He dropped to all fours, the forest ground slightly damp beneath his paws, scented with rich earth and other predators—coyotes, bobcats, feral cats, and dogs. Even skunks had crossed this area in the recent past. Nick welcomed the riotous odors overwhelming his senses, washing away Portia's fragrance.

Her face remained, eyes drinking him in, tempting, loving.

He tore through the brush, unworthy of a present and future with her, sickened by the past. His last moments with Bree, his mate and wife, would torment him until he ceased to exist. He'd promised to protect her always and had failed miserably.

She'd died in his arms, her throat torn away by a she-wolf from a vicious horde that had attacked their pack. He'd been so focused on helping Derek battle the opposing Alpha male, Nick hadn't noticed the shifter behind him. Bree had attacked the much larger wolf. The creature's mate had run to his rescue, determined to stop Bree.

She hadn't had a prayer. His fault no matter what Derek and the others had claimed. Nick's one job had been to see to her safety. Such a small thing to do or expect, yet he'd fallen well short of what a man or shifter should do. With her mortally injured, he'd cradled her close and lied to himself, wanting to believe everything would be all right. Shifters healed quickly. He simply had to get her to an emergency room, let the docs fix her up, giving her a fighting chance. She slipped away before he could move her from the spot, the light in her eyes dimming, life escaping on her last breath.

Before she'd gone, her eyes had filled with tears yet she'd smiled and mouthed, I love you.

That night he, not she, should have died. If he could only have those moments back, sacrifice his future for hers....

Too bad fate didn't work that way.

Unable to hold in his anguish any longer, he stopped and unclenched his jaws to howl his rage and agony. Wolf scent stopped him from making a sound.

Nick shuddered, his sorrow turning to concern. He lifted his snout and sniffed, not smelling Portia.

Relief washed over him, yet wariness remained, his hackles raised. He swept the moon-washed landscape. A large, gray wolf hid within the mottled foliage. Nick's pulse jumped. The creature eyed him carefully. From its scent, a male and shifter, though not just one of Nick's kind.

Kent.

What he was doing out here was a mystery. Kent lived in town, close to the store he owned. Although he was in admirable shape for a man in his mid-forties, he didn't seem the type to take moonlight runs as exercise or for the hell of it. Holing up in his office, counting his cash, seemed more in line with his personality. Word had it he'd screwed his business partner big time, forcing the man to leave the area, giving everything to Kent. A couple of girlfriends had faced similar exits, used and abused. The guy was an ass.

Nick braced himself for his approach.

Ears pulled in, Kent drew back into the shadows and sank to the ground. A subservient position.

Not wanting to prolong their meet, Nick leaped across a fallen tree and took off, putting distance between himself, Kent, Moonlight, Portia, memories. Forest streamed by, the landscape smeared from his speed. One mile lengthened into five and more. The distance didn't help. Escaping the past was as impossible as changing his eye color.

He stopped and howled until his lungs burned and his throat hurt. Ignoring the pain, he yowled repeatedly, pouring out his helplessness and grief, but not coming close to exhausting himself.

Unable to go back, he ran into the darkness ahead.

***

When Nick returned, the community was quiet, lights off except for Portia's kitchen washed in a warm, yellowish glow. He should have gone home and knocked back a six-pack to sleep. Perversely, he slipped behind an oak, spying on her like a lovesick teen.

The window framed her perfectly. She bent her head to the sink, hair glossy with reddish highlights, shoulders drooped.

His fault. The knot in his chest thickened and

twisted, bringing a shitload of deserved pain.

She fiddled with something then looked up suddenly, her gaze seeming to touch his. A pulse thumped in his temples, his urge to run intensified despite the unlikelihood of her having seen him. As shifters, their hearing was phenomenal. Some, not all, had eyesight much better than humans. Even with her backyard bathed in moonlight, she couldn't see through a tree trunk to him.

She lifted her face and sniffed.

Smelling him was another matter. Her scent had already enveloped Nick.

In another moment, she might come outside and call his name. What then? Give into his relentless need for her and spend the night only to wake up with the mother of all sexual hangovers? Or do the right thing and leave her alone so she could find a decent man, shifter, whatever she required. Someone without his baggage who could make her happy.

He wanted nothing more than to see her smile. He would have given up several decades of his life to kiss her hurts before she covered them with Band-Aids. Neither was a workable option. He dug his thumbnail into the trunk, stalling.

She left the sink and didn't return. Before she rushed out the back door, he slipped through shadows, taking a circuitous route to his bungalow, the interior no more than five hundred square feet.

Tonight, the space overwhelmed him with its unbelievable emptiness, her scent not as strong here. Bree's was only a distant memory, fading more with each day.

Troubled, he lumbered to his bedroom and fell on his mattress, fully clothed, begging for sleep, not expecting an answer to his foolish prayers.

***

Well before dawn, Nick installed the linoleum he'd left the previous day. A project he completed in the faint glow of camping lights with the shades drawn to avoid detection. Portia was an early riser. Every few seconds, he stopped and looked over, expecting her to be in the doorway, giving him a dimpled smile, making him want all over again.

Drained and edgy, he made too many mistakes,

cutting the flooring short, nearly slicing off a fingertip. He sucked the cut until it stopped bleeding then tried to focus, take more care.

By eight a.m., he'd sliced up his hands pretty damn bad, the heat sucked, and the air was beyond syrupy. He tied a blue-and-white kerchief around his forehead to keep sweat from stinging his eyes.

His friend Ty strolled in, ready for work. "Morning. Whoa. You look like shit."

Just what he didn't need. The man's blunt comments.

Nick pounded a nail into a board, hoping Ty would do the same in another room, preferably in another cottage.

The goon rocked on his heels. "So, who're you supposed to be with that thing on your forehead? Johnny Depp from Pirates of the Caribbean? A banger?" Ty contorted his fingers into pseudo gang symbols and danced around like a gorilla. Given his shock of red hair, freckle-stuffed face, and gangly limbs, he looked more ridiculous than usual.

Nick lifted his hammer. "How would you like a free lobotomy?"

"Bad day already, huh?"

He muttered an oath.

Ty leaned in. "You have a bad time with Portia last night?"

The hammer hit wood rather than the nail, barely missing Nick's thumb. "What?"

He crowded Ty, who skittered back, banging his shoulders against the wall. "Hey, take it easy. I was only asking."

"Did Portia talk to you?"

"No."

"Then why in the fuck would you ask such a stupid question?" Oh hell. Nick clenched his teeth. "Were you in her backyard last night?"

"No, but it was hard to miss you guys heading there. If your face gets any redder, you're going to explode. I can guess what happened between you two. Wasn't it good? Wait. It was too good, right?"

Nick cursed himself for having opened up to Ty in the past, admitting his shame over Bree's death, his decision never to fall for any woman again. "I'm not going to talk about this. Don't ask. Don't even think about it. Ever."

"Hey, I've never been obsessed about your love life or lack of it. You want space, that's cool. You want to talk, I'll listen. That's all I'm saying."

"I don't want to talk." He returned to his work, pounding nails. His ears rang from the noise. Before long, his blisters had blisters. Fran and Olive, two older shifters, dropped by, complaining about the din that had gone on for hours.

Nick mumbled an apology but kept busy, slapping white paint on the wood as quietly as possible.

Ty whistled from across the room. "Time for lunch."

"You go. I'm not hungry."

"Sure?"

"Yeah, Mom, I am."

"Your funeral, but you haven't stopped since I got here."

"I'm not tired." He slouched against the unpainted wood, stifled a yawn, and drew his brush sluggishly over the wall. After he was done here, he'd lay other flooring, work on some roofs, cut a few lawns, dig up plants then put them back and start over again. Anything so he'd sleep tonight. Hopefully, the dreamless variety.

"Nick?"

Portia.

He turned so quickly, his brush sprayed paint across the floor, barely missing her work boots.

Today, she had on yellow-and-white polka dot socks, no lace. She hadn't worn her overalls either. Instead, she sported white cut-offs, the super short kind that barely reached past the tops of her thighs. Several strings dangled down them. He tore his gaze away. Her yellow blouse had tiny sleeves that fluttered in the scant breeze and sported a neckline that dipped low on her chest, giving him a promising view of her cleavage.

She smelled better than a pristine forest, the first hint of spring, and a cool shower on a scorching day.

He gripped his paintbrush, popping a blister.

She lifted her picnic basket. "I brought us lunch. Hope you don't mind. I wanted you to have the steak I promised."

Behind her, Ty lifted his reddish eyebrows. A muscle jumped in Nick's jaw, his molars aching from gritting them. Ty put his screwdriver on the floor.

"Think I'll take lunch now. Later, guys."

He fled.

"This is looking great." She turned a slow circle, taking in his careless paint job, bent nails, tools tossed carelessly aside, the spattered floor.

He squeezed the bridge of his nose.

"Oh no." She hurried to him. "The paint."

Nick glanced over. "Where? What about it?"

"On your face. You touched your nose, and your fingers had paint on— Oh my God, what did you do to your hands?"

She grabbed both, unknowingly squeezing his cuts and blisters. At the surprising pain, he sucked in a breath.

She stared. "You're hurt."

"Occupational hazard."

"Since when? Were you working with your eyes closed?"

He'd been daydreaming about her. Dumb move. He pulled back his hands. "Nothing wrong with me."

"What about the paint on your nose?"

He looked down it, not seeing anything.

"Here, I'll get it off before it dries." She daubed his

face with a lacy handkerchief in pale yellow.

Her fragrance blanketed him, driving away coherent thought. Before Nick lost what little sense he had left, he grabbed her wrist. Bad move. Her softness and heat threatened to undo him. It took monumental effort to keep from hauling her into his arms. Speech was equally difficult. "Stop. You're going to ruin that."

"I can get others. You can't imagine the bargains on eBay and Overstock.com."

He laughed. "That where you get your socks, too?"

"You don't like them?"

He could spend a lifetime watching her model those babies while she wore nothing else except a sultry smile. "They're cute. Don't let anyone tell you different."

She beamed, carving a deep dimple in her cheek. "I wasn't planning to. We can't eat in here. Looks great, but the paint odor kind of gets to me."

He couldn't smell anything except her.

"How about we go to a spot between our houses? We can sit on the grass and dip our feet in the stream just before it goes underground."

Water was a definite hazard when they were together. Too much temptation urging them to strip and cool off. "You'll get grass stains on your shorts."

"I have OxiClean White Revive. Works great. If I weren't such a chicken, I'd use it on my teeth rather than those expensive treatments."

Jesus, she was something. Definitely not his future. "I should keep working. I probably won't be hungry for hours."

She glanced at his growling belly.

Fuck, when had that started?

"Sure you don't want anything I brought?" She stroked his stomach.

His cock sprang to attention, wanting out of his jeans and briefs, in order to slip into her hand, mouth, cunt, even her anus if she'd allow that. "You didn't go to a lot of trouble, did you?"

She circled his navel. His legs wavered. "Trouble with what?"

"Lunch."

"Just some steak sandwiches with sautéed onions, Parmesan-garlic mayo, provolone cheese, Italian seasoning, and Worcestershire sauce stuffed between a butter-grilled hard roll, along with home fries, cole slaw, applesauce, and southern baked beans on the side. So no, I didn't."

He lowered his face to hide his smile. "You not only fix pipes but can cook, too?"

"I'm great at watching TV. Mainly Rachael Ray's 30 Minute Meals and Sandra Lee's Semi-Homemade shows. Thank God for cable or I'd have to scour YouTube for recipes and demonstrations. I'm not an expert, so you tell me how this smells."

She opened her basket.

Scents nearly as delicious as hers encouraged him to inhale deeply. His mouth watered so badly, he practically drooled. "Wow."

She slipped her arm through his. "Let's get our table."

***

Okay, so she was running him down like a rabid cop fixated on an FBI Most Wanted suspect. Portia couldn't help herself. No, that was wrong. She didn't want to stop. Waiting for Nick to come to the right conclusion about them could take forever. Even if it were mere days, she didn't want to lose any more time.

When he'd left last night, she'd never been as cold even though the day's lingering heat and mugginess practically smothered her. With him, her nudity was natural and right. Once he'd gone, she couldn't pull on her clothes quickly enough. She'd wanted to run off her anxiety but lacked the energy, barely shuffling inside her house. TV, computer games, and the Internet had annoyed, making her restless. Finally, she'd scrubbed her place from top to bottom, ending in the kitchen.

Exhausted and lonely, two things hit her at once. The same awful odor from before and Nick's scent.

His delicious fragrance had vanished faster than their respective orgasms. Reluctant to go outside and sniff her property like a rutting she-wolf, she'd dragged to bed, tossing until dawn...possibly around the same time he'd been laying linoleum. This morning she'd seen his handiwork, guessing he was either the most dedicated employee on Earth, loved to do flooring, or he'd wanted to dodge her. That fucking hurt, but strangely enough also made her determined not to let him do that to them.

Someday, he'd appreciate that.

She squeezed his hand, thanking him for carrying her basket. He laced his fingers with hers, no hesitation, a natural reaction. Reckless with joy, she steered him to their destination. Watery light drizzled through trees. Vegetation drooped in the insufferable heat. The puny breeze failed to stir up anything, including dust. An undeniably shitty day. She couldn't have been happier.

Stopped at the spot, she was ready to boogie. Even in full daylight, this place was isolated from prying eyes. Exactly why she'd chosen it.

Nick studied the ground. "There's nothing but dirt here. You'll get your shorts dirty."

Not if she ditched them and everything else as she'd planned. "I can toss them in the wash."

"Or I can do this." He pulled off his tee, smoothed it over the ground, and gestured to what he'd done.

His muscles bunched and flexed with every move, stealing her breath. Dark, silky hair peeked from his pits. Simply awesome. "You want me to sit on your shirt?"

"That's the plan."

"It'll get dirty."

"But your shorts won't." He offered his hand, helped her down, and unlaced her right boot.

Him undressing her was unexpected and nice. She'd assumed they'd tear off their own clothes, as they'd done last night, and get to the main event with no time to linger on flaws. God knew, she wasn't perfect. Losing five pounds wouldn't kill her. More runs in the woods would tone her muscles the way they should be. Thankfully, she'd touched up her toenail polish earlier. This morning, she groomed better than she ever had, her bikini line pristine, legs smooth.

With great care, he laid her sock on his tee then traced her tat. Giggling, she pulled her foot away. "That tickles."

"Yeah?" He gripped her ankle and ran his fingers up and down her sole.

She screeched and fell back. "Stop. I can't stand it."

"Bad, huh?"

Too spectacular for words. She grinned, loving this. He looked hot and adorable, his powerful chest, biceps, and shoulders making her weak. Paint streaks on his face urged her to cuddle him. "Do it again."

"Not if you holler. Fran and Olive already bitched at me for hammering too loud."

"Pooh on them. Next time they need their pipes cleaned, I'm going to overcharge."

His shoulders shook with laughter, his face so red it practically glowed. "Huh?"

She flushed at what she'd said. "You know what I mean."

"But will they?" He removed her other shoe and sock.

Portia hoped he wouldn't have too much trouble with the laces on her blouse. If he ripped them off to get to skin, she wouldn't mind.

He took off his boots and socks then dunked his feet in the water. "Aw God, that feels good."

Them naked on his tee doing the nasty would be even better. She sucked her lip, reminding herself not to push. Small steps might be best and the only option available at this point besides the food.

49

Every woman had heard the sage advice about the way to a man's heart.

She filled a plastic plate with his sandwich and sides, each mound larger than the last. "Here you go."

He swatted at a bee. "Did you save any for yourself?"

Food wasn't what she needed. "Sure."

He peered into the basket, then piled half his portion onto a new plate, and handed it to her.

"You don't trust my cooking? You want me to taste this first? If I don't gag, you're safe?"

He scraped a blob of cole slaw from her thigh, where it had fallen, and licked the food off his fingers.

She leaned close. "Good?"

He finished chewing, swallowed then scrunched his face. "Shit."

"What?"

His eyes rolled up. He slumped to the ground.

"Oh my God, what's wrong?" Couldn't he eat mayo? Were carrots or sugar poisonous to his system? Good God, she didn't know. They were from different packs. "Nick!"

She shook him.

He laughed. "God, you're easy."

Damn right, but only with him, and he wouldn't take advantage. She slapped his shoulder. "That wasn't funny. I thought I'd poisoned you."

"Naw." He pushed up and grabbed his sandwich. "But we'll see."

Portia eyed him carefully, smacking him every time he pretended to choke or cough. Finally, they both settled, digging into her feast. His satisfied grunts matched the sounds he'd made last night while making love to her. They hadn't merely screwed. They'd connected.

"Damn, this is good." He shoveled in more applesauce and beans.

She bumped his shoulder with hers. "You like, huh?"

"Fuck yeah. You have a little...." He wiped something from her bottom lip and sucked it off his finger.

"Thanks. You have some...." She leaned over, tonguing Worcestershire from his mouth.

The persistent bee buzzed near. Ignoring it, Nick kept close. So did she, smoothing back his hair, tucking the strands behind his ear.

They sagged to the ground, not caring about the dirt or bugs, their lips brushing, kisses searching. A far gentler exploration than the last time, but enormously satisfying. She breathed him in. He did the same with her. They made out like adults who'd rediscovered sex. No rush. Easy. Slow. Seductive.

She cupped his balls and stroked his cock, making it rise beneath the rough denim. How delightful. He slipped his hand under her blouse and bra, claiming what was his, because she'd willingly given herself to him. Her nipples tightened painfully, her very being aching for everything he had to offer.

Nick mounting her was the only conclusion she'd accept, along with them sharing their lives. They rocked in place with her finally rolling them over and straddling him.

Sharp knocks rang out.

She jerked. He looked over.

The knocks sounded again, a fist hitting wood. "Portia. You home?"

Ty's shout surprised her. Nick pulled down her bra and top, swung her from his lap to the ground then lifted his face. "Over here. What's going on?"

By the time Ty had rounded the vegetation, she had on her socks. Nick shoved on his boots.

Ty gulped air and pointed over his shoulder. "I just came from Matt's bungalow. Fran was straightening up."

Yeah, so? Fran did housekeeping to earn money. Everyone here had a job, whether it was construction-maintenance in the community, running the general or convenience stores, Moonlight Diner, or working with Derek at The Defenders, a security agency. Portia couldn't figure out why Ty was so agitated. Water dampened portions of his jeans and tee. "Is something wrong?"

"Fucking A. I heard Fran shout. She must have just turned on the water in the bathroom. It was shooting to the ceiling when I got there. The pressure blew off the knob or handle, whatever you call it. The thing struck her between the eyes. There's blood everywhere."

Chapter Three

Fran wasn't a gentle soul when she was in a good mood. For Portia to catch her at a time like this....

The older woman sat on the commode, rocking and moaning like a victim in Hostel or any number of Saw flicks. Her salt-and-pepper bob was wet and tangled, clothes soaked. She pressed a wad of toilet paper to her forehead. Blood snaked down her prominent nose, the skin beneath her eyes already blackened.

With her being a shifter, the injury would heal swiftly though not instantaneously. Definitely not fast enough for Fran.

Despite the water-soaked floor, Portia sank to her knees, trying to remain calm, forcing herself to be exceedingly gentle, too. At this point, no one needed more turmoil. "Did you lose consciousness? Can you see all right?"

Fran sobbed, deep, wrenching sounds.

Crap. "Maybe we should take you to the ER, have them check you out, get some X-rays."

Her shoulders trembled.

"Fran?" Portia touched her knee.

The woman reared back, teeth bared. "Stay away from me. Don't you ever put your filthy hands on me." She punched Portia's wrist.

"Hey." Nick sloshed through water. "We know you're upset, and with good cause, but there's no reason to act like that. Portia's only trying to help."

"How? By killing me? I said get away." She kicked her foot, forcing Portia to crab back. Fran's expression got uglier, her upper lip curled. "You're either too dumb to know how to do your job or you did this deliberately to hurt me."

"What? No. I would never try to hurt you or anyone." Portia got to her feet, her eyes stinging with tears. "This has never happened to me before. I installed the fixtures correctly. I don't know what could have gone wrong."

"I do. You don't belong here. You're not one of us. You'll never be one of—"

"That's enough." Nick stood between them. "It was an accident, all right? Stuff happens."

"Not to me. Not before she came here."

"I'm sorry." Portia wrung her hands, not knowing how to fix things between them or how this could have happened. It was nuts. Handles didn't shoot from sinks like projectiles, except in cartoons or horror films. "Maybe the part or screw was defective."

Fran leaned over to see around Nick. "Only one thing's not fit to be in Moonlight and that's you."

He growled. "Knock it off."

"No. Someone needs to tell the truth around here."

Portia bounced on her heels. "I wasn't trying to hurt you or anyone. I'm sorry. I'll pay for your ER visit. I'll do whatever you want."

"How about you leave for starters? Why are you still here where you're not wanted?"

She'd never been wanted anywhere. Moonlight had been her one chance to belong and be accepted. What an idiot she'd been. She ran from the room.

"Portia, wait!"

Nick called again, but she bolted out of the cottage, stopping abruptly. Three female pack members stood near the steps that led to the porch, their expressions concerned or wary. They stared at her face then her blouse.

Blood streaked the material. She had no idea how it had gotten there.

Inside, Nick and Fran argued, her comments shrill and accusatory, his so low, Portia couldn't make out the words but they were curt with anger, defending her, an outsider, refugee, someone who'd never belong.

She dashed from the scene, racing into the vegetation. Leaves brushed her legs, branches whipped her torso and arms. The sting scarcely registered. Dappled green turned dark and uninviting, the area shadowed from the heavy sun, not allowing the smallest thread of light or hope inside.

What had seemed such a promising afternoon had turned hideous so quickly. No different from the day her parents had died. They'd left to go grocery shopping. A routine trip that should have taken less than an hour. After two hours had passed without their return, she'd called their smartphones to see if they'd stopped at their favorite diner for lunch before getting the other food. The call to her mom went to voice mail. A gruff voice answered her dad's phone, the man identifying himself as a cop, asking who she was.

She hadn't wanted to say, afraid to know why he, rather than her parents, talked to her.

Portia's attempt to duck reality hadn't changed what had already occurred. The driver who'd T-boned her parents' car had been texting and walked away without a scratch. Lucky her. She had two kids at home who needed their mother.

Portia was an adult who could easily take care of herself. She had. Finding the pack, begging them to take her in, craving nothing more than a sense of belonging with kindred souls who wanted and loved her.

She dodged bushes and trees, putting distance between herself and pain. Wasn't enough. She tore off her blouse and bra, tossing the garments aside, not caring where they landed. She had to change and keep running. Returning wasn't possible. She'd never be able to forget Fran's disgust, the others' wariness, or Nick's sweet protection that could cause the pack to turn on him next.

Oh God, no. Not that. He'd lost so much already.

An anguished sob caught in her throat. She staggered to a stop and ripped off her shorts, thong, boots, and socks. Before they hit the ground, her transformation began. The surrounding air stilled and the world blurred, like an image seen through a rain-washed window.

Within seconds, it was over and she ran on all fours.

She darted into the undergrowth, not caring about her direction, escape her only goal. When she didn't return, the pack would be relieved. Nick, too. She'd pushed him too hard. If he hadn't been such a good guy, he would have told her to knock it off. They'd never had a chance. She'd been a fool to think otherwise.

Running hard, she changed directions. At her advance, a cottontail rabbit froze. Portia veered to the right to avoid hitting the poor thing, having caused enough destruction. As she passed, the creature zipped to the left, spared to live another day.

Others of its kind wouldn't be as lucky. She'd have to live off the land from now on, staying clear of humans and other shifters. There wasn't a single place she'd ever belong. Another fantasy she shouldn't have hoped for.

With a wolf's eye, she took in the surroundings, knowing this area would never do for her home even though there were plenty of hiding places and game to feed on. Staying here would put her too close to Nick, his scent permeating the air. She shot through the foliage, determined to travel hundreds of miles, if need be, to stop smelling or thinking about him.

Her sides ached from the exertion, lungs burning. No matter how far she ran, he still seemed to be everywhere.

She collapsed and rolled onto her side in human form, naked and miserable, knees pulled to her chest, lids squeezed to hold back tears. They dampened her face, throat, and chest in great gushing waves she couldn't stop. Between gasps of air, she cried herself out, grieving her parents, her stillborn relationship with Nick, her sorry future. Never seeing him again was too terrible to consider, the same as her trying to survive. She might not find another pack. Even if she did, there was no guarantee they'd want her either.

That left her with living among humans, struggling to fit in as she had when her mom and dad were alive. Not something she wanted to do after living in Moonlight.

She rocked worse than Fran had, unable to make a decision or plan.

A twig snapped.

Portia jerked to a sitting position, skin crawling at the possibility of a hunter approaching, assault rifle in hand to prove what a badass he was. Although humans didn't normally roam this area, there was always a first time.

To the side, leaves rustled wildly. A large, black wolf broke through.

Nick.

He transformed within seconds as she had, arms held out, inviting her within his embrace.

Tears clouded her eyes, rolling down her cheeks.

She wanted nothing more than to lose herself within his protective heat but pushed up and edged away.

He followed. "Everything's all right. Come back with me and you'll see."

"No. They want me gone."

"That's not true. Fran's Fran. If anyone's lucky to call Moonlight home, it's her. She probably drove her mother nuts with her constant bitching. Just because she mouthed off, doesn't mean—"

"What happened could have killed her. I would have been responsible."

"It was an accident. Shit happens."

"Not that. Not to me. You shouldn't have talked to her like you did. Now, she'll hate you, too."

"And I should care, why?"

She flapped her hands. "Moonlight's your home."

"Yours, too."

"No. I can't go back. You heard her, I'm an outsider. I'll never belong."

"Bull."

"Everyone hates my guts."

"Not me." He gathered her into his arms, stroking her back.

Portia slumped against him, tears streaming down her face. She hated herself for being so freaking emotional. Hell, she was a damn fool for touching him. This was crazy wrong, but she couldn't find the strength or courage to stop.

They kissed, their desire eager and hungry, his breath still scented with Italian spices, hands roaming her ass, dipping to her cunt and breasts.

She pulled free and sank to the ground.

"Hey, what are you doing?" He reached for her. "Get back here."

"In a sec." Okay, more than that. She needed lots of time to do what she wanted. With his balls cupped in one hand, she held his hot, hard rod in the other.

Nick sucked air, his long toes splaying then curling.

His pleasure didn't begin to touch upon what she'd desired for months. Never had she known a more spectacular man. His musk enthralled her. His warmth was thrilling. His rigid cock and fleshy sac were sinfully wicked. No normal woman could have resisted his male allure. Portia couldn't begin to try.

His nuts rested heavy and hot in her palm, stoking

her desire. Gently, she fondled his sac and swirled her tongue over his beefy crown, dipping the tip into his small slit. His salty pre-cum tasted better than anything she'd ever had. His groans were pure delight, lover's music she'd longed for.

They shouldn't be doing this, or at least, he shouldn't. Good sense demanded he run from her without regret, giving his loyalty to the pack, including Fran. Not a newcomer. Worse, an interloper.

Rather than putting distance between them, Nick pressed closer. Rarely had Portia experienced such acceptance. He gripped her head to keep her near.

There wasn't anywhere else she'd rather be.

She took his cock into her mouth, opening her throat so he could tunnel deep as he would in her pussy. He cried out. She suckled, drawing him in, not satisfied until she'd reached the root, her nose buried in his dark curls. Musky. Male. Magnificent. She squeezed his ass, pleased at his taut cheeks.

He dug his fingers into her scalp.

With a gentle sweep, she tongued his length, easing back gradually, finally trapping his crown between her lips. Slavishly, she explored his satiny flesh, gradually travelling toward the back. There, she flicked her tongue on the uneven skin.

He shuddered. "Fuck."

In time, even though they shouldn't. Somehow, doing the sensible thing seemed unimportant here. They'd claimed this area as their world, a slice of heaven she'd fight to keep. Pleasuring him mattered more than anything.

Portia parted her lips, allowing his rod to slip free.

"No, wait. Don't stop."

Never. She guided his shaft aside and eased his left ball into her mouth.

"Holy mother fucking shit."

Yeah, she ruled. He did, too.

***

Hot didn't adequately describe her mouth, while her tongue.... Damn. Wanton as hell, sweeping over his hairy ball, delivering pleasure every-fucking-where, even his lashes and nails. Nick shivered, not certain he could withstand the delight. For him to come now would be worse than his rod going limp. He had to hold off for at least ten minutes. Okay, five. Maybe two.

Argh.

She suckled his nut carefully, stroked his shaft hard and quick with piston-like precision, and brushed the furrow between his cheeks, pausing to toy with his anus.

He wanted to scream, cry, come. No. For her, he had to last longer than any guy on Earth, prove he was the man, and could do something right. He hadn't scared Fran one bit. Despite his repeated warnings to the old bat, she'd still run Portia off. If he couldn't prove himself here, he wasn't worth a damn.

Portia slipped her finger into his tight ring and turned her digit, familiarizing herself with the passage.

His legs sagged. Sweat dripped from his chin to his chest.

She suckled his nut more firmly, though not enough to harm. His hair stood on end, vision blurring. Unexpectedly, she released his ball and panted hard. He couldn't snatch one meager breath.

Dizzy, he dug his toes into the dirt and plowed his hands through her hair, holding tight.

"You doing okay?" She patted his leg.

"Uh-huh. You?"

"Great." She took his rod back into her mouth.

Jeez-us. Florida summers had nothing on her inner heat, her fervent embrace precisely what he needed. He understood that now. Witnessing her sorrow and loneliness from Fran's ruthless bitching had been more than he could bear. Until that moment, Nick hadn't understood how unwanted Portia felt. How lonely she was. He'd been nicer than Fran about pushing Portia away, but he'd also behaved as cruelly. Not opening his heart to her, even refusing to be friends.

They were more than that, had been since the beginning, no way could he keep denying that truth.

Unable to flee any longer, he delivered himself to her lusty care, lost in her fragrant warmth. She worked his shaft in and out of her mouth, a soft, feminine sound escaping her.

He tilted his chin to the forest canopy, eyes closed, surrendering his will to whatever she desired. One lick became two and more then a flick, her tongue teasing his most sensitive area. Dazzling pleasure surged through him, draining his resolve to hold off. He clamped his jaw and resisted climax, running construction quotes through his head, adding extra to Fran's job, then concentrated on tools and materials, not the delight rolling from his cock to his belly, chest, and thighs.

He locked his knees, tensed his legs, bit the inside of his lip.

Portia gently squeezed his balls.

Nick's mouth sagged open, a howl tearing through the forest. From him? Must be, though he couldn't recall having made a sound. He tried to breathe but his chest was too tight, his lungs worn out. Too bad. He had to hang on for a little while longer.

Release hit with tsunami force, his cum spurting into her mouth. Oh shit, he had to stop. He didn't want to gross her out.

Lightheaded, he staggered away.

Portia yanked him back, gripping his ass, drinking his cock dry. Honoring him. More importantly, accepting who he was, flawed as fuck, barely worthy of her.

Finished, she licked his crown and looked up. "Still good?"

If he'd had the strength to laugh, he would have. "Yep." The world spun, taking him with it. He dropped to the ground, his knees ramming hard.

"Oh God." She grabbed his upper arms. "That must have hurt."

His afterglow was too intense to allow pain. Later, he'd probably be limping. "I'm good." He slipped his arm around her waist and dragged her with him to the ground. "I'll be ready to go again in a sec."

She stroked his nipple. "That long?"

He laughed. "Unfortunately, I'm not Superman."

"No?" She suckled his throat.

Felt good until it stung. "Ow."

"Sorry." She rubbed his hurt.

Not as great as her mouth, but he wasn't going to complain. "Were you giving me a hickey?"

"I got carried away. I'll behave from now on."

Who said he wanted that? "Just say you'll come back to Moonlight and we're good."

She curled into him.

After her second sigh, Nick tightened his arm around her waist and slung his leg over hers. "I hope you're not thinking of taking off while I snooze."

"I should."

"Fuck that. The second we wake up, we're going back. You belong with the pack as much as I do."

She didn't argue. Nor did she nap. Neither did he, afraid to close his eyes, guessing the moment he did, she'd dash away. This time he might not be able to find her without discarded clothing giving him a heads up as to which direction she'd taken. As always, her scent seemed to be everywhere, so pervasive it confused and enticed.

He rubbed her arm. "Tired?"

"I could sleep. Go on. Nap."

"You first."

Breathing hard, she rested her arm over her eyes.

"Guess that means we should head back."

"You go on. I'll catch up."

He eased her arm away so she had to look at him. "Are you planning to be as stubborn as I was?"

"What are you talking about? When did you stop?"

He hugged her hard. "The moment Fran opened

her big mouth and made you cry."

"She did not."

"Fine. You have brass balls. You can chew nails and spit tacks. You can—"

"Let's say we talk about what I can't do. Apparently, even the simplest plumbing job is beyond me."

He pulled back. "Do you honestly believe that?"

"Hell no. I'm good at what I do. Whatever happened in that bathroom is not my fault. I installed the damn thing correctly."

"Then let's tell Fran that."

Portia made a face. "Would that be in between her making me feel like a leper?"

"She was out of line." Nick figured Satan would have trouble with the old biddy. "I told her so and that she'd better not do it again."

"Bet that shut her up."

She'd kept hollering well after he left the porch. "If you let her run you away, you'll have nowhere else to go."

"I'll manage."

"I won't."

Portia's expression changed. Hope, caution, doubt, and what might have been fear crossed her lovely features. "I don't want you screwing up your place in the pack for me."

"It's not your call, and I won't. Come on." Despite his fatigue, he labored to his feet and offered his hand. When she didn't accept his gesture, he leaned down. "Give me trouble, and I'll sling you over my shoulder to carry you."

"Why are you doing this? Is it because you feel sorry for me?"

So many emotions swirled within him, pity couldn't have possibly squeezed its way inside. "You're a braver person than I'll ever be. A far better one, too."

She slapped his hand. "Don't ever say that or even think it."

"Keep reminding me and I won't." He pulled her to her feet and into him. "Time to go back, under your own power or mine. Which do you prefer?"

She tried hard not to smile, but still made a small dimple. "I'm already responsible for you popping the blood vessels in your eyes and risking a hernia. No way am I going to add a slipped disc to that."

"Wow, maybe I should use a fallen branch as a cane, or we could build a wheelchair to push me back to the community."

"Stay here and I'll rent one for you."

He towed her back and smacked her ass playfully. "Stay in Moonlight. Please."

She rested her forehead against his shoulder. "I hate when people don't like me. I've never been popular, but reviled is worse than what I faced with middle-school bullies."

"Fran talks big and loud. But what happened isn't as bad as you think. She'll calm down."

"Maybe." Portia wrapped her arms around his torso. "If I agree to go back would you do me a favor?"

"Anything except packing a U-Haul with your stuff."

She laughed softly. "Once we're there, would you mind if I wait at my place while you get the parts that messed up? Before I see Fran or anyone else, I'd like to go into town and talk to the jerk I bought the holder from."

"Kent."

"What— Wait, who?"

"The guy who owns the store. I'll drive you there, get the new parts, you'll replace them, we'll make sure everything's okay and then go out to dinner, a movie, whatever you want."

She stared. "Like a real date?"

"Sure. I'll pay and everything."

Wonder flooded her face. "Thanks."

He kissed her gently, his tenderness surprising but not disturbing him. He enjoyed the emotion. "Thank you."

"For what?"

Giving him countless chances to understand what Bree would have probably told him if she'd been able. That she'd want him to be happy, to have what they'd once had, to love again. He'd never forget her. He'd always remember how he'd failed. Only now, he'd do better, cherishing Portia, protecting her with his life, always keeping her safe.

He brushed his lips over hers. "Thanks for everything."

***

Portia couldn't stop grinning or horsing around with Nick. She smacked his ass. He tickled her relentlessly. Both of them laughed until they neared Moonlight. She held back, stomach churning. Nervously, she fingered the ripped laces on her blouse.

Nick glanced at the bloodstains then pulled off his tee, handing it over. "Wear this. I'll grab a new one after I get the damaged parts. Stay here, all right?"

She nodded.

He pecked her mouth. "Everything will be fine."

Hopefully. She paced while he was gone, his absence seeming to take forever. Pack members were busy with their daily routines, not spotting her. Ty suddenly strayed close to the forest edge. Portia ducked behind an oak. He didn't look over, concentrating instead on the lumber he carried.

At last, Nick returned, wearing a fresh white tee, the paint scrubbed from his face, his hand out. "This look like what you need?"

She fingered the handle and other materials.

"Yeah. Was Fran still there?"

"Nope. She's probably out riding her broom."

Portia laughed, surprised she could.

On the way into town, they listened to Keith Urban, Lady Antebellum, Faith Hill, and Tim McGraw, then strolled hand in hand into Kent's, a utopia for plumbers and construction workers, countless aisles stuffed with every conceivable material and tool.

Nick lifted his arm immediately, flagging down a tall man in jeans and a dark-blue tee, his hair more gray than blond.

She leaned close. "That's Kent?"

"Yep."

He was a good-looking dude, except for his smile not reaching his eyes. Goose pimples rose on her arms. Suppressing a shiver at the sudden cold, she lifted her face to the ceiling vent, chilled air pouring down. Should have felt better than it did.

"Nick." Kent shook his hand. "What can I do for you?"

"Not me. Portia."

She showed him the defective part, explaining

what had happened.

He screwed up his mouth. "This is what you get when everything's made overseas. Give me a sec and I'll get you a new one. No charge, of course."

"Thanks."

"You bet."

Nick squeezed her hand. "Told you everything would be all right."

She leaned close so the other shoppers wouldn't overhear. "Why don't you like him?"

"What? I never said I didn't."

Nick's frosty expression had given him away, unless she imagined things. "He kind of puts on, doesn't he? Like, he's not really as nice as he pretends."

"He's a businessman. Comes with the territory."

True. "A shifter, too." She'd caught his scent.

"Yeah, he was—"

"Here you go." Kent hurried down the aisle, materials in hand. "These just came in. If you have any trouble, let me know."

"We will." Nick escorted her from the store. "How long will it take you to install that?"

"Shouldn't be too much time, why?"

"We have a date."

Right. Smiling, she climbed into his pickup, an old model Nick told her he'd saved for and tended lovingly. "You were going to tell me something about Kent when he returned."

"I was?" Nick drove from the lot and shook his head. "Can't recall what it was. Maybe it'll come to me later. While you fix the sink, I'll finish painting the cottage wall. We'll meet at your place after that, all right?"

"Absolutely. Should I wear something fancy?"

He patted her thigh. "I like your pink socks with the lace."

She had dozens. "Then I'll wear them. Anything else?"

He stroked a string from her cut-offs, touching more skin than material, heat radiating off his fingertips. "Surprise me."

Totally doable. Suddenly, she couldn't wait to get back, wanting him to floor this baby.

He drove carefully, almost too cautiously, but at last Moonlight came into sight.

Portia had just left the cab when Ty ran up, his complexion as red as his hair and freckles. Bile rose in her throat. "Is Fran okay?" Good God, she couldn't have died. "Did she pass out? Has anyone taken her to the doctor?"

"She won't go." He swallowed hard, snatched some air, then looked from her to Nick and back. "She told Derek what happened. He's called a meeting and wants you there."

Chapter Four

Pack meetings took place in Moonlight Diner. The establishment closed after luncheon crowds left so the crew could prepare for the evening rush. With the midday meal past, shifters, rather than travelers, filled the chairs and counter seats. Nick tightened his arm around Portia's shoulders, encouraging her inside.

She didn't want to be here.

With her reluctant approach, quiet conversations ceased, everyone's attention swinging to her. Some in the pack looked curious or surprised at Nick's embrace and show of support, others wary as they concentrated on Portia alone. Fran and Olive were downright hateful, their chins lifted, looking down their noses at her. The gash on Fran's forehead had already scabbed, the dark circles beneath her eyes lightened somewhat. Despite the improvement, she hadn't calmed down, as Nick had asserted. Her homely features tightened with disdain.

When Portia had been in middle school, her principal wore the same look, his face stony with scorn, whenever classmates blamed her for something they'd done. Breaking school property, smoking in the john, stealing money from a teacher or student. No matter how many times she'd proven she wasn't responsible or what they'd claimed wasn't possible, Mr. Jeffries kept ordering her to his office, blaming her for taking up his precious time, warning that she had better behave or face suspension, possibly expulsion. By the time she'd reached high school, Portia had policed her every move, afraid to breathe too loudly fearing someone would call her on it.

It seemed nothing ever changed, no matter how many years had passed or whether she was with her own kind or not.

With no chairs or stools left, she and Nick stood near the locked door. So did Ty. He squeezed her wrist in sweet encouragement. Her eyes teared.

Derek sat in the back next to Rand, a tall blond who was second in command. Their features didn't register to Portia, Mr. Jefferies' scowling face replacing theirs.

Derek rapped the table. "Let's get started."

Nick tightened his grip on Portia's shoulders. If he hadn't, she might have run, her pulse already racing, making her shaky.

On a loud grunt, Fran pushed to her feet, mouth twisted in rage or pain. She clutched the table as an arthritic would, using the furniture to stay upright.

She'd had no trouble kicking at Portia in the bathroom or smacking her hand. Now, she was suddenly an invalid?

"You see what she did to me." Fran glanced around the room, making certain everyone got a great view of her battered face. "If I hadn't jumped back when I had, the metal could have pierced my brain and killed me or put out an eye. My vision's still not too good. I don't know if it will ever go back to what it was. The pain is awful. It's everywhere."

She ran through a litany of her aches.

When she'd finally wound down, Olive patted her wrist. "Tell them what happened when you tried to shift."

"That's right. Thank you, I almost forgot."

Nick huffed.

Fran played to her audience, brown eyes widened. "The change took longer than it ever has, even when I was a child and first learning to shift. I've never had any discomfort before, but now I do. I can barely stand the shooting pains in my legs and shoulders."

"Shouldn't your nose and forehead be giving you the problems?"

With Ty's question, everyone looked at him. He lifted his shoulders. "Well that's where the thing hit Fran. Seems only reasonable that's where she'd hurt the most."

Olive folded her arms beneath her sagging breasts. "There's nothing reasonable about this. We know she did that to Fran."

"Bullshit." Nick released Portia and stepped forward. "It was a fucking accident."

Olive stiffened, her expression appalled. "How dare you use that language with me or contradict what I say."

"Someone has to."

"I expect an apology."

"For the damn truth?"

"Nick, wait." Portia joined him. "I can handle this." What was happening here wasn't his battle. Not any longer.

"Handle it how?"

His worry touched her. "Please back off."

"You're sure?"

"Yeah, I am." Having been everyone's scapegoat for too long had finally fueled her fury to an impossible level. She didn't care what anyone's motive was in behaving so abominably, whether they were driven by wanting to feel superior, self-righteous, were wary of a refugee, or simply loved being mean. Right now, so much anger raged in her, Portia couldn't stop shaking.

She faced Fran. "I'm good at what I do no matter what you claim. I'd fixed that sink properly with materials I got from Kent's. Nick and I were just there. Kent as much said the piece was defective. We all know the junk that's coming from overseas. Pet food that poisons dogs. Defective drywall and copper plumbing. The handle that struck you is simply another in a string of problems with those imports."

"So now it's someone else's fault. Sure. That's what all guilty people say."

"No, that's what I'm saying." She strode to Fran, getting in her face. "If you doubt me, ask Kent."

"He runs a store. He's no expert."

"Neither are you."

"Get away from me." Fran swung her foot then her arm.

Portia stepped back. "Wow, it's a miracle." She gestured to Fran's leg and hand. "Did everyone see that? She can move just as easily as she always has."

Olive stood. "We want you out of Moonlight immediately."

Those words should have terrified Portia. Too much adrenaline pumped through her to allow any fear or backing down. "Why do you want me to leave? Because of an incident that you damn well know was nothing more than a freak accident, or for the real reason—I'm not exactly like you. I'm not one of the original pack." She turned to the others. "When I first came here, I recognized a community that pulled together and protected its members from the outside world, because each of us is different. Humans would certainly say we're abnormal or cursed. So, we're going to be like them now, picking each other apart for perceived deficiencies? Fine, let me get the ball rolling."

She focused on Olive and Fran. "How old are you two in human years? Fifties? Sixties? That's really getting up there. How can the pack thrive with old members who can't move as quickly as the rest of us or have trouble shifting?" She gestured to Fran. "You just admitted as much."

Fran slammed her fist on the table. "Because of what you did to me. Before that, I had no problems."

"You're sure? Want to see if you can shift as quickly as I can? Bet you can't. With each year, you'll have more trouble. Eventually, you'll slow down to the point where you'll need help to shift, walk, do your daily chores. Happens to everyone when age creeps in. You're not special. So what should we do about you, Olive, and others when that happens? Leave you in the forest to starve so the young, strong members can build the pack? Let you stick around but do nothing to help you out since you're not valuable to the pack anymore? And what about him?" She gestured to Ty. "Look at that red hair and those freckles. He's the only one here like that. Should we push him out too because of his coloring?"

One by one, she targeted each pack member, except for Derek and Rand, pointing out their differences, none of them perfect.

Okay, Nick was. When Portia finally got to him, she stopped.

His eyes sparkled with pleasure, pride at what she'd said registering on his features.

Olive had already plopped in her chair, head down at having the tables turned on her. Fran jabbed her finger at Portia. "This isn't over."

"Yes, it is." Derek stood. "The material was defective. That's the long and short of it. Let's get back to work." He strode from the room, followed by Rand, Ty, and the rest. Olive and Fran left through the kitchen, muttering furiously.

Nick hugged Portia. "Damn, you were amazing."

"More like pissed."

"I had no idea you had that in you."

"Now you do. So watch it, mister. Cross me and you'll get the same."

He nuzzled her ear. "I like when you talk dirty."

She giggled and wreathed her arms around his neck. "We still on for our date?"

"Even those two old bats wouldn't stop me. Fix your sink, I'll paint my wall, and we'll meet at your place after we clean up, okay?"

"We could stay there. I'll cook, save you the money."

"No fucking way." He rocked her back and forth. "Tonight, you relax and enjoy, while I show off my girl."

Her eyes grew moist. She smiled so hard her cheeks hurt.

***

Nick slapped paint on so fast, specks flew wildly, dotting his arms, tee, and jeans.

Ty chuckled. "Big night planned?"

Hell yeah. He'd been perfecting this evening's

program since leaving the diner, wanting their date to be the best Portia had ever known. She wasn't only brave but wise, everything she'd said ringing true. Olive and Fran had never been quiet for so long, color draining from their faces after Portia mentioned their ages. A sore spot for any female, whether she was a shifter or human. He guessed they hadn't liked how the pack members kept bobbing their heads in agreement to Portia's comments, riveted by her words. Damn. She didn't have brass balls. Hers were made of steel.

He dipped his brush in the paint and gave Ty a sly grin. "None of your business."

"Lucky man."

"You have no idea."

"You won't either if you don't get a move on." Ty jabbed his thumb at the window. "Portia just shot past, heading for her place."

"Was she smiling or crying?"

"Grinning from ear to ear, Fran nowhere in sight."

Shit. Portia had already finished her job while he still had a fourth to go on his. "I hate to ask...."

"Go. You deserve a good night. I'll finish up."

Nick clamped Ty's shoulder. "You're a good friend."

"Damn straight. Even though you're getting paint on me." He knocked Nick's hand off.

Laughing, he patted the man's freckled cheek, leaving paint there. "Have fun."

"Yeah, you too."

He would. Nick groomed himself as he hadn't in too long, taking care with brushing his teeth, shaving, showering, scrubbing paint from his arms and hands. His cuts and blisters had already healed. Without thinking, he slapped on his aftershave, a leather scent Bree had liked. Hopefully, Portia would feel the same.

Once he'd dressed in his best knit shirt, new black jeans, and cowboy boots reserved for weddings or funerals, he checked himself in the bathroom mirror. Joe Manganiello he wasn't, but Portia seemed to like him. That's all he cared about.

He plucked wildflowers from his yard and snatched some nice looking roses from another pack member's place, since that shifter and his mate were at their respective jobs. With the area deserted, no one spotted him behaving like a douche. Somehow, it wouldn't have mattered if they had.

He held the bouquet to his chest and rapped once on Portia's front door.

"Nick?"

"Yep."

"Coming."

They'd both be before the evening was over.

She swung open the door, stared at him not the flowers, then sagged against the jamb. "Wow, you're gorgeous."

He couldn't find adequate words to describe her. She'd worn her cute-sexy socks as promised, pairing them with white high-heel sandals. Her dress was unexpected, making him damn near orgasmic. Narrow ribbons served as straps, each tied into a pert bow on the top, the neckline dipping low to reveal the valley between her breasts. The pink-and-white striped fabric hugged her like skin before flaring at the waist to a full skirt that stopped several inches above her knees. Her legs were smooth and tan, the dewy flesh bearing no moles or freckles, only the amazing rose tat on her calf.

His testosterone shot up so fast, sweat clung to his

neck, back, and chest. "Please tell me you have on a thong."

"Sorry, I don't."

Crud. "One of those really tiny panties?"

"You mean bikinis?"

"Yeah."

"No."

Damn. "You wore one of those girdle things?"

"What? No." She smacked his biceps then leaned in, her breath clean and hot against his cheek. "Nothing. Nada. No underwear at all. I couldn't find any to match my dress."

Glory hallelujah. "Are you trying to kill me?"

"I could ask you the same. Sure you want to take the time to go all the way into town when there's food here?"

If not for the dessert part of his plan, he would have caved. "Yeah. Let's go. Wait. These are for you." He gave her the flowers. "Oh hell, are you going to cry?"

"No." She flapped her hand in front of her face and blinked away tears. "These are beautiful. You shouldn't have."

"It was no biggie."

"No, I mean, you really shouldn't have. Valerie and Zach didn't see you stealing their roses, right?"

"It'll be our secret."

"You bet." She pressed her nose to the blooms, inhaled deeply, and sighed. "Nice. Smell."

He snuggled his face to her neck. "Amazing."

She giggled, sniffed then stilled. No, she stiffened.

Fuck, she didn't like his aftershave. He eased back, not surprised to see her nose wrinkled, upper lip curled. "I can wash it off. It'll only take a sec."

She regarded him blankly. "What?"

"My aftershave. You don't like it. That's fine. I can wash it off."

"Wait." She grabbed his arm before he could run to his place. "It's a leather scent, right? I love it."

"Sure? You didn't look that way."

"I smelled something else." She shook her head. "It's gone now."

Nick looked over. "Was it Ty? Last whiff I got of him nearly knocked me down."

"No. Not Ty. Doesn't matter." She tapped the flowers against his chest. "We better take off before anyone else notices how you stole roses and weeds."

He fingered a tiny white petal. "These aren't flowers?"

"'Fraid not. But at least they're not poison ivy."

"Does that affect shifters?"

"Dunno. I'd rather not find out."

Right. He helped her into his pickup, piled in, and took off.

She rested her hand on his thigh, precisely where she should. "Where are we going?"

"You'll see."

***

He pulled up to a mega-nice restaurant on Gulf of Mexico Drive, the narrow land area surrounded by water, a balmy breeze tempering the heat.

This place had to cost a fortune Portia figured Nick didn't have. She squeezed his hand. "Are you wasting next month's rent on this meal? You shouldn't."

"I'm not. I'm enjoying myself. Aren't you?"

She threw her arms around him. "This is the nicest

time anyone's ever shown me."

"We haven't even started."

He requested a patio table, after asking her if that was what she'd like. They could have eaten in the parking lot and she would have been thrilled. Sailboats skimmed the placid water, wind snapped the bright blue umbrella above their table, palm leaves swished. The hostess and server were all smiles, both women eyeing Nick. Portia couldn't blame them. He put Charlie Hunnam to shame. However, if either woman made a move, she'd rip them apart. No more cowering for her. She was a kickass shifter.

For appetizers, she and Nick chose Portobello mushrooms, along with chips and salsa, feeding the fare to each other. He suckled her fingertips. She licked his palm, not caring what the other diners thought.

The server recited an endless entrée list of fish, each on special tonight. Although eating seafood wasn't unheard of for wolves, they settled on New York strips with the trimmings. She gave the server a smug smile. "We like meat. Rare. The fresher the better."

Nick bumped her leg. She bumped back. They snickered.

The steaks arrived, grilled flawlessly. Seared to perfection on the outside, each forkful juicy and red.

He swallowed bite after bite, barely chewing the food. "We need to set up a restaurant like this in the forest."

"No kidding, with the patrons running down their own meat. Think of the bucks that'd save on the chow we'd have to order and kitchen help."

His shoulders shook with laughter. "I can hear Fran now, complaining that someone else got the best carcass." He made his voice nasal and whiny likes hers. "Derek, Derrrrr-rek, that was supposed to be my meat. I want to call a meeting. I want everyone to clear out of Moonlight."

Portia covered her mouth, quieting her giggles. "Maybe she's the one messing with the plumbing, wanting the other places for herself."

"She sure as hell hates when I pound nails."

"That settles it. I'm getting you an industrial-strength nail gun so you can go to town day and night."

Nick raised his fist in a power salute. "Right on. Wouldn't it be cool if you could hook up a Behemoth hit to it and make the nails shoot out in time with the beat?"

"Great idea. Plus having massive speakers."

He bounced in place. "Surround sound, too."

"And laser lights."

They gave each other a high five, and collapsed with laughter, their glee turning to chuckles then happy smiles.

He kissed her fingertips. "Having fun?"

"The best ever."

"It gets better." He pointed his fork. "We haven't had dessert yet."

She leaned close. "Are we still talking about food?"

He winked.

***

After leaving the restaurant, Portia waited for Nick to pull off into a wooded area. There, they could shift, run, and mate to top off a great meal and evening, with that being the perfect dessert. Given their fledgling relationship, her fantasy might be a tad premature. Even though they'd known each other for months, during most of that time they had shared no more than longing gazes. At least she had, with him always hurrying away.

No longer. He finally landed on the same page as she was.

However, wolf-to-wolf mating represented the greatest commitment for shifters. A bond neither of them should take lightly.

Better not get her hopes up. Even if he'd only planned to buy her a Baskin-Robbins ice cream cone, that would be okay with her.

He drove into a resort parking lot and shut off his engine. Like the restaurant, this place was on the water and uber nice. Color her stunned and confused. "We're going to a free seminar where they'll talk us into buying timeshares?"

"Nope."

"There's a great band here with dancing?"

"You dance?"

When no one was looking. "Do you?"

"Guess we better take that off our itinerary."

"What's on it exactly?"

"Wait and see."

He registered at the front desk, thanking the desk person for the key card.

Portia pressed her mouth to his ear. "Please tell me you've fallen into an inheritance. Did you see how much these rooms cost?" When she'd read the brochure, her eyes had nearly popped out.

"It's only money."

"Where'd you get so much?"

"Working round the clock in the community and doing security work for The Defenders on the side. I haven't had anyone to spend my stash on. Now I do...don't I?"

Oh God. Without trying, she'd brought up Bree, Nick having been alone. "How far to our room?"

"We're on the top floor, ocean side. Miles and miles away. Think you can wait?"

"Hell no. Race you."

He pulled her back and swept her into his arms, as a man does with a bride. Two older couples applauded. Portia's face stung from excitement and pure pleasure.

Nick carried her from the lobby to their room, not putting her down by the door. "Can you get the key card?"

She pulled it from his shirt pocket and inserted it into the slender slot. Once inside, she was on him as fast as he was on her. Clothes flew in every direction with her having the advantage, not having worn underwear. His boxer briefs were still around one ankle when he stopped stripping and pointed. "Leave the socks on."

"Yes, sir."

They tumbled to the bed, making the springs squeak, devouring each other's mouths. He draped himself over her until she pushed him off and zeroed in on his neck, her mouth welded to him, lips suckling.

"Ow, ow, ow." He wiggled. "Another hickey?"

She hadn't finished the first one. "Sorry." She dove in for more, finally branding him with a mark that would hopefully last an hour. Damn shifter ability to heal quickly. The moment the blotch faded, she'd tend to it again. Lucky her. "Let's really play."

"Sure. Wait. Where are you going?"

Portia stopped crawling away and straddled his legs, her back to his front. She lifted her ass and scooted toward him until her pussy was above his mouth, his family jewels beneath her face. "Here. Is there a problem?"

Savage noises poured from him, a wolf ready for the rut. He grasped her hips and pulled her furry cleft to him. She dipped her head to his rigid cock and tight balls, the dessert he'd promised her.

They gorged on each other's sex, mouths pressed close, lips sucking, tongues dallying over flesh glutted with lust, heated with passion, desperate for release. No way would she rush, savoring his clean-musky scent, the leather hint she adored.

Back at her place, she hadn't meant for him to misunderstand her reaction, thinking she didn't like his fragrance. That other odor had suddenly intruded again. He still hadn't smelled it.

Why?

No. Screw it. Now wasn't the time to consider anything except his big body, rippling muscles, and thick, fragrant curls. She wanted to shriek with joy, but was too busy taking his cock into her mouth.

He growled and tongued her clit, licking her as relentlessly as she did him. They filled the room with pleasured sounds, their scents mingling with sexual fragrances. Male. Female. Life. Lust. She shuddered, desire spiraling then bursting, making her come too fast, unparalleled delight hurtling through her.

Her mouth hung open. She gasped.

Nick swung her off him, settled behind, and pulled Portia to her knees. "Spread your legs, lift your ass."

Only death would stop her.

He plunged his rod into her damp pussy, thrusting hard and deep, precisely as she liked. With each pump, he stroked her clit. She lifted her face and came again, harder than before, too freaking soon. Damn, damn, damn. After fighting for air, she rested her cheek on the bedspread.

Nick pumped away, playing with her boobs, nipples, clit.

Pleasure rocketed through her with breathless intensity. She jerked. "No. God. Give me a minute."

"Why?"

"I'm too..., This is.... I can't...." She pounded the

mattress, unable to make a coherent sentence.

"Want me to stop?"

"No."

"Good."

Gawd. He brought her to another climax, pulled out, and touched her anus. "Want to go for broke? Up to you."

There wasn't anything she'd deny him. "Yeah. Please."

"You ever do this before?"

He would ask. "No. But I want to with you."

"I'll be careful." He kissed her ass then used her lubrication and his seed to prepare her. "Ready?"

"Yeah."

He entered slowly, inch by glorious inch.

She gripped the spread.

He stopped. "Too much? Did I hurt you?"

Hell no. Never had she been as filled, stretched to the limit, the act wonderfully decadent. "Uh-uh."

"Uh-uh what?"

"You shouldn't have stopped. Why did you? Don't!"

"Okay, okay. Hang on."

He stroked her nub. She bucked and clenched her jaw, enduring the delicious torment, her ears buzzing. He panted, thrust, and teased her clit. She backed into him, wanting more, even though he was driving her loony. After another pump, he roared, coming with her.

They slumped to the mattress, still joined, arms and legs trembling, damp with perspiration, wrapped in warmth and wonder from their joy.

***

Nick couldn't get enough of Portia. If he lived an eternity, he still wouldn't have had his fill. After a brief nap, he peeled off her socks.

She opened one eye. "You don't like them anymore?"

"I love them. That's why I'm doing this."

"I see. No, I don't. As much as you like them, they're not going to fit you. You're a big guy." She ogled his stiffening shaft.

"Don't worry, neither of us are getting dressed yet."

He carried her into the shower then directed her to the wall. She slumped against the tiles. He lifted her hands to the rod that kept shampoo and other stuff from falling off the shelf. "Go on, grip it. Keep your arms up."

She regarded him through lust-slitted eyes. "Having fun?"

"Are you kidding? Getting you clean is work."

"The dirty variety, huh?"

Already, she knew him too well. He washed off first then soaped her good, paying particular attention to her nipples and cleft because he liked them so much. As far as her good heart, ballsy bravery, wicked sense of humor, and smarts were concerned...he was falling in love with the person she was, or maybe he was already there. Nick didn't know. She seemed to have always been part of his life. He didn't want to recall a single moment without her. If the pack had forced her to leave today, he would have followed her out of the community, keeping her close. Together, they would have found a place to belong even if it was only with each other.

Neither of them would ever be alone again.

He eased into her. She melted into him. Effortlessly, they fit. Beneath the gentle spray, she held onto his shoulders at the same moment he cupped her ass, pulling her up so his cock could slip back into her cunt.

Their lovemaking was more sensual than frantic. Oddly enough, also more impassioned. They burrowed into each other's core, reaching past facades and fun to their souls. He invited her inside his, their gazes caressing, smiles knowing and reserved for them alone.

They resisted climax far more impressively than they had the other times. Possibly lasting two minutes. Maybe a few seconds past that.

When Nick came, he pressed his face against her shoulder. She did the same with him. They clung to each other in the steamy heat, making the moment, the world, and everything else stand still.

Chapter Five

An uneasy truce settled between Fran, Olive, and Portia. The older women didn't speak to, look at, or bother her. She stayed far from them, too, taking extra care with her work. Handles no longer shot from sinks. There were no more kitchen leaks or bathroom flooding reports. All was right with the world.

Especially hers and Nick's.

Each day, they enjoyed lunch together, her surprising him with culinary treats she'd learned from the Food Network, or him bringing baloney-and-mustard sandwiches so she wouldn't have to do the work. A good guy. At night, they retired to her cottage or his, sharing the cooking and clean-up duties, after which they watched TV programs like an old married couple. She loved Grey's Anatomy, even with McDreamy's departure. Nick liked The Blacklist, Blindspot, and The Following, which he lamented for having been canceled. As long as the show was about a government conspiracy or wacko killers, he was on board. After the evening news, they retired to her bedroom or his for the real entertainment.

Since their date, they lived joined lives, more so than many couples who'd exchanged vows or had fully mated.

Shifting and running together remained the only thing they hadn't done. When Nick gave into his inner wolf, he preferred to do so at twilight. She favored the hours before sunrise. Moonlight and the surrounding forest always seemed cooler then. Plus, she never ran into another shifter during that time.

To come across Olive or Fran after their change wasn't something Portia wanted to do. She still didn't trust them completely. Seeing them naked while they shifted was too much punishment even for a masochist. That kind of stuff would make a wolf want to go blind.

She checked the nightstand clock. The day would

start soon. Disappointed, she nevertheless slipped from Nick's embrace. His upper lip fluttered with a mild snore. After easing his hair from his forehead, she kissed his eyebrows. He stretched briefly, his musky scent enveloping her.

She went limp with wanting. Maybe she wouldn't shift today.

He rolled to the side, his back to her. Fighting the urge to jump him, she tugged on denim cut-offs and a pink bra so she'd be nominally decent before slipping into the forest. She didn't bother with shoes.

Loamy soil and dewy vegetation perfumed the air. Crickets chirped. The cottages were dark, illuminated only by the three-quarter moon, its silvery rays making everything magical.

She inhaled deeply then quickly slapped her hand over her mouth, swallowing hard to avoid being ill. That same odd, sickening scent hit. She followed the stench to the forest edge across from Zach and Valerie's place. Portia craned her neck and sniffed repeatedly to determine where the foul odor came from or to spot an animal carcass rotting in the humid environment.

There wasn't anything out there, not even disturbed soil that would indicate a regular wolf had buried its prey, as they'd been known to do with surplus kills. Dogs followed the same pattern.

She couldn't detect either animal's scent.

The stench vanished, as it always did, replaced by a sweet rose fragrance. Troubled and mystified, she jogged to her backyard.

Rabbits and rodents scurried into the brush. Once naked, she bolted into the thicket, shifting rapidly. On all fours, she raced through the forest, gulping air, loving the endorphin rush from a hard run. Almost as good as sex.

Ashy beams lit her way, creating a wonderland no human had ever experienced. Mammals' eyes glinted in the faint light, the creatures spying her approach and departure. Insects crept across the path in a long unbroken line, one following the other on mindless instinct. Bats soared overhead, their leathery wings whapping the clammy air. Leaves rustled violently, more than they should from her having passed or the breeze disturbing them. The wind blew in her face, keeping her from detecting an unwelcomed visitor's scent from behind.

Panting, she slowed and turned, neck hairs raised.

Nick stood on the path, fully shifted, his black fur glistening in the moonlight.

Portia's heart caught. She wanted to believe this meant what she'd longed for but was too afraid to hope.

He approached first, a quiet whining noise pouring from his throat, the sound every wolf recognized as the start to courtship and bonding. Thrilled, she padded near, vocalizing as he had, giving herself to him for all time. They'd been born for each other. No one could convince her otherwise.

He mouthed her muzzle. She did the same with his. They touched noses, repeatedly bumping their bodies together. Beneath the gauzy light, they groomed each other's coats, nibbling the fur.

Nick bowed to her, tossing and tilting his head then laid his legs over her neck. If a wolf could have squealed with delight, Portia would have. She'd never known him to be such an outrageous flirt, using all his charm on her.

She'd been a goner the moment he'd first said "hi."

Getting down to business, he smelled her sex, flicking his tongue in and out, testing to see if she were ready. She had been, for more months than he could have guessed.

Her joy broke free, so did his. They nestled and nudged, then whipped their tails across each other's muzzles, their behavior instinctive and primal, as required as human wedding ceremonies.

Nick mounted her from behind, his sex piercing hers, delivering otherworldly comfort nothing had ever matched. He thrust rapidly, a wolf unable to restrain his shameless desires. She welcomed his beast, her sheath narrowing. His cock swelled, tying them together. What should have been their most vulnerable moments were protected and sacred, nothing daring to harm them.

At last, he twisted around until they were end to end though still joined.

There they remained, belonging to each other now for life.

***

Nick should have claimed her sooner. Coward that he was, he'd held back these last days, uncertain whether Portia would commit her future to him. Sure, she enjoyed his company, got down and dirty with him whenever he wanted, and spent every minute she could at his side. That didn't mean she was truly in love. To her, they might have merely been friends with benefits...the super great kind.

These last moments had changed everything.

Back to their human forms, they lay on the forest floor, facing each other, grinning from ear to ear.

He cradled her hand to his chest, confident in their future. "So who moves where now? You to my place or me to yours?"

"How about we keep both and build an addition to join them. Plenty of room for the kids."

He liked the way she talked. He'd been an only child, then lost his parents in a tornado. Having a large family had always been his dream—endless activity, noise, laughter, hope for the days to come. "Sounds great. With the extra jobs I do for The Defenders, we'll be able to afford renovations in no time. I'll work nonstop if I have to."

She stroked his pec. "And neglect me?"

"Never." He kissed her greedily, proving he'd be a fervent lover. She made sweet noises and slung her leg over his, grinding her pussy against his cock.

Lost in her embrace and warmth, he didn't rush, exploring her with tender care and wicked passion.

They snuggled closer.

Sun spilled across their bodies, the rays bleeding through a break in the vegetation.

Crap. Too much precious time had passed already. He wanted every second back. "Feel like playing hooky today?"

"Always." She suckled his neck, darkening his hickey, a favorite pastime. Oddly enough, what she did no longer stung.

Finished, she smacked his ass.

"Ow. What was that for?"

"Someone has to punish you for tempting me."

"In that case, you'll always be beating me up."

"Only now." She stroked his butt. "Though I'd love to ditch work today, we can't. I got stuff that can't wait. So do you. Aren't you helping Ty fix the roofs?"

"He probably won't notice I'm missing."

"Until he does. Then he'll pound on my front door until everyone in the community knows we're in the bedroom banging our brains out."

Nick pulled her into him, snuggling his shaft against her cleft. "We could do it in the shower instead, or why don't we just stay here?"

"I understand Fran likes to take morning runs. If we're lucky, we might be able to see her shift. Maybe Olive, too."

Ew. "Better go." He got to his feet, hauled Portia to hers, and slung her over his shoulder.

She shrieked.

"Quiet." He paddled her. "Do you want to wake the natives?"

"Listen." Country music floated on the breeze. "I think they're already up."

Even with her added weight, Nick hotfooted it to her shorts and bra. When he'd left, he hadn't bothered with clothes. Maybe he'd build a thirty-foot wall around their joined houses so they could frolic nude without worrying about the others.

With him and Portia protected by brush, no one could spot her dressing or him checking the community. Several members were already gone, on their way to pack businesses. Lights illuminated cottage windows. Ty shuffled from his place, stretching, yawning, scratching his underarm.

Despite the distance, he spotted Nick immediately and called out, "Good, you're up. Let's get to this."

"I'm not ready yet."

"I noticed. How long will it take you to finish peeing on Portia's property, scent marking it?"

God. If anyone heard that, Nick would never live it down. Fran might call another meeting to discuss his disgusting habit, despite that being a natural wolf instinct. "I haven't had breakfast yet."

"Well, hurry up. I want to finish before it gets really hot."

The air was already dank, hazy sunlight promising to make it worse. "See you in a few."

Portia grabbed Nick's hand, leading him into her bungalow. "Come on, I'll make you something to eat. How about ham and eggs, pancakes, home fries, biscuits, French toast—"

"Whoa. We're going to have to wean you from cable food shows. It'd take me all day to eat that."

"I see the problem. Want me to heat up some Pop-Tarts?"

"Let's not lose our heads. Go on and do your thing. Ty will have to wait until we're through eating."

Nick pulled Portia toward the shower.

She resisted. "The kitchen's behind us."

"I thought I'd lather you up first, then you can do me, then I'll do you."

"How about you go ahead while I cook? A more efficient use of time."

"Not as much fun."

"True." She stroked his rod. "But we still have lunch and all that time after dinner."

"Forever. Please, promise me."

"Nothing will keep me from you."

They hugged fiercely, made out like sex-starved teens, then finally broke free, padding in opposite directions.

By the time Nick had washed and dressed for the day, glorious aromas drifted from the kitchen. Grilled sugar-cured ham, each slice with a crunchy edge, fried potatoes and onions, biscuits or maybe bread giving off a faint yeasty smell. He sniffed so much he felt dizzy. "You're going to spoil me."

"You get to do the dishes."

"I knew there was a catch." Once she had their plates on the table, he pulled out a chair for her then sank to his.

They enjoyed the bounty, too ravenous to speak. Nick finally wagged his fork at her. "You should seriously consider opening your own restaurant. This is great."

She licked yolk off her lip. "What about the diner? Wouldn't want to go into competition with them. Hey, wait. I could pick up some hours there to make extra cash for our renovations."

"No."

"No?" She pulled back, forehead furrowed. "You won't give me your permission?"

"I didn't mean it like that and you know it. I don't want you working twenty-four-seven, just like you don't want me to. We need time for each other."

"We could always work in the diner together."

"I can't cook. I don't want to learn either. If food doesn't come fully prepared, I'm not interested."

"Maybe we could work some security details

together."

"Absolutely not."

"Come again."

He held up his hands. "I don't want you getting hurt."

"I don't want that for you either. You can't take any more of those jobs ever."

"What? They only involve guarding construction sites so no one steals copper wiring or other stuff."

"Sounds easy and safe. Even I can do that. In fact, I insist. Now it's your turn to be all Alpha again, telling me no. Go on."

He hung his head. "Is this our first argument?"

"More like a disagreement. Want to make up?"

Laughing, he pulled her onto his lap. "We'll work this out, okay? If you do go with me, I want you to wear a helmet, goggles, bulletproof vest, body armor—"

"I'm not going to get hurt and leave you, I promise."

"Baby, you can't know that."

She held him as tightly as he did her. "Let's both find other ways to make extra bucks, all right? Surely, we can work security without it being dangerous. Like investigating stuff on the Internet. We see it all the time in your programs."

"That's Interpol, the FBI, CIA, and the rest of the alphabet agencies."

"So? We'll start small. Stuff we can do together from here. Okay?"

"We can try. Where do you think you're going?" He pulled her back onto his lap.

"I was shooting for my chair. Your food's getting cold."

"So is yours. We can eat it together from here."

They kissed more than anything, laughed, too, their quarrel already forgotten.

Nick grabbed the last biscuit, putting it on her plate. A loud crash sounded outside, followed by a brief yell.

He and Portia tore from the cottage, zooming toward the noise, the same as other pack members, Olive and Fran included. Fran sneered at Portia's cut-offs and bra. The rest had stopped at a bungalow two buildings down, a ladder resting against the outside wall. Its roof had a gaping hole that hadn't been there earlier.

Nick dashed across the front yard. "Ty!"

"Wait." Portia grabbed his arm and used her weight to keep him from tearing free. "Be careful."

"I will. Let go."

Once she had, he ran into the cottage. Dust rained down, along with something else he couldn't immediately identify. He swatted and coughed. "Ty! Talk to me."

The guy's foot and leg had crashed through the ceiling.

"Ty!"

He moaned.

Nick ran outside, nearly colliding with Portia. They both reared back. She gripped his hand. "Is he all right?"

"He's alive. I don't know how injured he is." Nick hauled the ladder inside to bring Ty down from the ceiling access door. Pulling him out of the hole and across the roof might make the whole damn thing collapse.

A male pack member hollered, "What happened?"

"I don't know. Help me."

The guy and three others rushed to Nick. Once in the crawlspace, he inched toward Ty, wood groaning beneath his weight. Sun slanted across the confined area, dust swirling in the rays. They shone on the beams, honeycombed with damage. Nick jerked his hand away from a termite swarm in the thousands, many falling through the ceiling past Ty's leg.

His arms were scraped and bleeding, face pale.

"Ty."

He blinked slowly and winced, his face crumpling. "Shit."

"Can you move your fingers?"

"What?"

"Can you move?" Fuck, he couldn't be paralyzed.

After what seemed a lifetime, Ty finally lifted his arms and pulled his free leg up.

"Hold it." Nick put out his hand. "Careful with your other leg, it broke through the ceiling."

"What the fuck happened— Holy shit." He brushed bugs away. "What are these?"

"Termites."

"What? No. Impossible. We sprayed."

That they had, only a few months ago. The wood

had been fine then, the poison supposedly first rate, with an added bonus. It had no odor. No different from using nothing more than water.

Frowning, Nick crawled closer, stopping repeatedly to test the wood. "Can you pull your leg up?"

"I think."

"Do so carefully then grab my hand."

The process took forever, but at last he guided Ty down the ladder, the other pack members helping him to the floor. Other than Ty's sprained ankle, bruises, and cuts, he seemed intact.

Joining them, Nick swatted his hair, brushed his shoulders, and smacked his clothes knocking off termites.

Portia crossed the room, cringing at the insects and sidestepping them as well as she could. "How did these get here? Didn't anyone spray?"

"You bet we did."

"The stuff didn't work?"

"Apparently not." In Florida's hot-humid temperatures, the insects had a perfect climate to reproduce rapidly and destroy just as fast. The only good thing about this was no one could blame Portia for what had happened. She hadn't been responsible for the treatment, nor had she purchased the chemicals. Another pack member had, with him spraying the cottages, too. Every single one. Which meant they were all possibly damaged or he'd missed this place somehow.

Nick wasn't certain what to think. "We need to check the other buildings. See if termites screwed them up, too."

Everyone agreed. Fran stood in the doorway, frowning at Portia.

The old crone had finally gotten on Nick's last nerve. "What?"

She shot him a snotty look and left. He sensed another meeting coming up. Fuck. "Let's go. We have a lot to check. Not you." He stopped Ty before he could leave with them. "Portia, can you help him to your place? Give him the rest of my breakfast?"

"Absolutely. I can cook more. Whatever he needs."

"How about a cane? My ankle hurts like hell."

Nick directed a male pack member to help. With Ty's arms around the guy's shoulders and Portia's, they brought him out to the porch. The others followed Nick to the next cottage to check for damage.

***

After Portia had cleaned Ty's cuts and wrapped his ankle, he polished off half a dozen eggs, the remaining biscuits, and four ham slices.

He belched. "'Scuse me."

"No problem. As an invalid, you're entitled to be crude."

"I gotta move in here. Please. I could get used to this." He leaned back, balancing his chair on two legs.

Portia grabbed his tee, yanking him forward. "Careful, please. Speaking of which, did the termite spray come from Kent's?"

"Probably. Wherever it came from, it sure as hell didn't work."

Like the faulty handle, and earlier, the pipe Portia knew for certain she'd fixed. "Maybe we should start buying our stuff from Amazon or at another store."

"Same stuff there as at Kent's. Never had a

problem before."

Yeah, weird. She sat next to Ty. "Do you think Fran's doing this?"

"Doing what?"

"Causing the termite problem, the sink handle, the other stuff that's gone wrong."

"No. Why would she?"

"To get rid of me."

He grew thoughtful then shook his head. "You work on plumbing, not pest control. If she did mess with the chemicals, she would have had to do that before you even got to the community, since we sprayed well before you joined us. Even if what you said is possible, the question is why? Especially with the roof. She doesn't hate the shifter who lives in the cottage I was working on. Far as I know, they're friends."

"Would anyone else here want to sabotage the work or the community?"

"To what end?"

She had no idea, except this many accidents in such a short period simply didn't make sense. Worse, the incidents were growing increasingly dangerous. If the ceiling hadn't held, Ty could have crashed through to the floor, broken his neck, and died.

Who'd want him dead? Wait.

Everyone here knew Nick was doing roofs today. Maybe he'd been the real target because of her, which circled right back to Fran.

Portia stood, ready to strangle the woman. Just as quickly, she dropped back down. Fran was the proverbial witch, but she wasn't psychic. She had no idea Portia would show up or live here.

Ty leaned in. "You okay?"

She wouldn't be until Nick returned.

Took him a while to check the other cottages, including his and hers, but he'd only found one other place damaged. Unfortunately, it was Fran's.

Despite their differences, Portia sympathized with the woman's problems. "Karma's a bitch."

"No kidding." He washed his hands at the kitchen sink. "Now, Ty and I have to fix her walls and floors."

Ty rested his head on the table. Portia patted his shoulder in sympathy. "Will she be there while you guys do the work?"

"Not likely." Nick grabbed a paper towel. "She's

staying with Olive."

"Did the shifter who sprayed forget to do her place and the other one?"

"He swears he didn't."

"Were there any chemicals left?"

"No. He used everything then disposed of the containers."

"Do you think this was an accident? Another one in a few short weeks?"

Nick's expression darkened.

Rather than further discuss her misgivings in Ty's presence, she coaxed him to the sofa. With a full belly, he fell asleep quickly, allowing her to pull Nick outside. "I don't want to be paranoid, but unless Fran is doing this because she hates me and wants me gone, then someone else might be."

"Who? Why?"

"The only one I can think of is Kent, since everything that's screwed up here is from his store. As to the why...remember that pharmacist who diluted cancer drugs to make more money on them? Maybe Kent's watering down bug spray or swapping out good merchandise with old stuff he's found, cleaning it up, hoping no one notices and he can rake in extra cash."

"Even if he is crazy or greedy enough to do that, why would all those tainted products end up in Moonlight suddenly? He'd have to be messing with everything he sells in order for us to get so many damaged things. If he did that, surely someone else would have noticed by now and he would have been shut down or sued."

Yeah, averages. The numbers weren't there for bad luck happening only in Moonlight. "Any reason he'd want this community gone? Do you know anything about his background? Where he grew up? The pack he came from?"

"I don't think he has one. I've never seen him with another shifter. Hell, humans don't like him either. He ran his partner off and several women. They were here one day, gone the next, never to be seen again."

"They disappeared?"

"I don't know. I just assumed they left town and stayed away because they hate him."

Kent's pasted-on smile and cold eyes might be one reason. He'd hit Portia wrong from the start, giving her an idea what she should do. "Be extra careful from now on, all right? Try to buy your materials from another store."

"He's the biggest in the area for specialized stuff. The pack's store doesn't have a hundredth of what his does."

"I know. But whatever you have from his place, check it out carefully before actually using it."

Nick rested his hands on her shoulders. "What aren't you telling me?"

She didn't want to get into it until she'd checked out her growing suspicions. "That I love you and don't want you hurt like Ty or Fran. Think you can do that for me?"

He pulled her into his arms. "I'll be good, promise. Want to come and watch me work? I'd love an audience."

"Let me take care of Ty first. Once I roast a cow and peel two or three sacks of potatoes for his lunch, I'll catch up with you."

He laughed. "You'd better."

***

With Ty asleep and Nick away from the cottage, Portia fired up her computer and researched Kent, getting a zillion hits. Most dealt with his business. Once she'd established that Walt Lucas had been Kent's partner, with Walt leaving the business quite suddenly, she searched his name. According to a people locater site, he'd relocated to Georgia.

On a whim, she called his number.

The line rang once. "Hello?"

She stilled, not knowing what to say. "Ah, hi."

"Who is this?"

She'd blocked her number from being displayed.

"What are you selling?"

"Nothing. I'm Portia Danes. I went to Kent's the other day and I have to say, I'm really disappointed. You were his business partner right?"

"If you're thinking about suing me, you're out of luck. Bastard screwed me out of every cent he owed."

"I'm sorry. I'm not trying to sue anyone. My mom and dad owned a plumbing service. Danes Speedy Repair. Ever hear of us?"

"Yeah. You guys do good work."

"Did. My parents died and I had to close the place. I'm still in plumbing, but I've noticed the products Kent sells now are shoddier than they'd been before. Did you do the buying when you guys were partners?"

"Why?"

Good question. She couldn't come right out with what she needed to say, preferring to dance around it, until Walt gave her an opening. "I was thinking that if you did, you could recommend a better store? Can you?"

"You called me for a recommendation? Don't you have a computer, sweetie? You can check out Yelp or Angie's List. Surely your folk's business was listed there."

She rubbed her forehead. "They were. Let's just say I trust you more than online reviews. We all know they can be bought. Not that my parents ever were."

He named two places. "Prices are slightly higher but you can trust them."

"Thanks. How about Kent?"

"What about him?"

"Can I trust him?"

"To do what?"

God, this was going to take forever. Time to get real. "Do you consider Kent dangerous?"

"What? Wait. Did he threaten you when you complained?"

"No."

"Then that only leaves you dating him. He finds most of his girlfriends by coming onto them when they need help with materials. Wish you would have called me before you decided to hook up with him."

"I haven't. Has he hurt his former girlfriends?"

"Why would you want to know that?"

"I'm worried about them. It's not like I can ask him."

"Why not ask them?

"Please answer me."

He breathed hard. "If I were a woman, I'd call him Prince Alarming rather than Charming, you know?"

"Can you tell me their names, all the ones you know about? I'd really like to talk to them."

"I don't know…. How can I be sure he's not behind this, using you in the hopes of suing me for slander?"

Poor guy was more paranoid than her. "Record me while I talk. That way he can get me for slander, too."

"How's that?"

"Because I'm saying I think he's killed someone."

Chapter Six

To Portia's surprise, Walt didn't gasp at her admission, call her crazy, or hang up. His calm acceptance spoke volumes. He must have believed Kent capable of murder.

She recalled the man's icy stare and dead eyes. "Were there any domestic violence calls on him?"

"He's too careful for that. I did see bruises on the girls. They acted intimidated, too, when I happened by them and him in the store or at restaurants. None of them would look at me. They stared at him like they were waiting to get the okay to breathe. As to physical injuries, it wasn't like they were sporting black eyes, but there were marks on their arms; what they'd get if he'd squeezed them hard or maybe punched them. A couple of times, there were scratches and scrapes on their wrists."

"Like he tied them up?"

"I suppose. Of course, it might have been them playing kinky sex games. Who knows? I wasn't about to ask."

"The women never confided in you?"

"God, no. They were meek, young, too, in their early twenties, easily conned and intimidated, if you get my drift. I would have loved to see him pulling his macho act on older women. They would have flattened him. Young girls without money are the best targets, especially when a father figure gives them attention. Boy oh boy, did he ever. Most of them had been in the store to get roach repellant. They all lived in pretty dicey places. He must have seemed like a godsend at first, showing so much concern for the shitty apartments and jobs they had, making up for that by taking them to nice restaurants, buying them clothes. I'm sure him telling them how to dress, act, and think probably got old after a while. That's surely when the trouble started with him insisting and them resisting. Gotta happen, you know? As the years passed, he got cockier, not trying to hide his temper or possessiveness. He spent a lot of time in the office, tracking them by phone or monitoring GPS when he should have been working."

"He put tracking devices on their cars?"

"Just like you see on cop shows. He wanted to know where they were at all times. My guess is they hadn't a clue what he'd done."

Her stomach cramped. "What happened to them? How'd he explain their absence?"

"He didn't, at least not to me. He'd be in the office one day, fuming over what was on the tracking device or after he'd spoken to them by phone, and the next day they were gone, along with anything that reminded him of them. It was like he'd flicked some kind of internal switch to make them disappear from his memory. Within days, he'd start prowling the store again, getting friendly with the new babes. Not that he was faithful to the ones he controlled when they were still around. While he monitored their every move, he'd mess with other women, some of them becoming his next victims."

"How many are we talking here?"

He made a pained sound. "There were dozens,

sweetie. In and out of his web like it had a revolving door, though there were three that lasted the longest."

"Do you know their names?"

"Sure. Spotted them enough when he spied on them on his computer. There was Trish Quinn, Marie Jacobs, and Brooke Kennedy."

Portia keyed the info into her computer. "Who came first, middle, last?"

"Brooke and Marie then Trish. Things were going bad with Trish before I left. With him losing his grip on her, he tried his shit on me, nitpicking every single thing, telling me what I should and shouldn't do. Right. I couldn't stand it anymore and wanted out, which is probably what he was shooting for all along. Greedy prick. God knows how many women he's been with since her...Trish. Don't want to know and don't care."

"Did he act unusual during any of the breakups? Nervous, sad, anything out of the ordinary?"

"Hell no. He has frost in his veins, not blood. It was like they'd never existed to him."

"Do you know where they lived?"

"You mean before they moved in with him? Those kids didn't have enough dough to go anywhere except the lousiest places in town. Real roach motels." He gave her the names.

"No one ever came around looking for them?"

"Not to my knowledge. I don't think the girls were connected with family like regular folks are. I heard from a checker at the store that Brooke had been in foster care most of her life, so her ties with relatives were most likely tenuous. If the SOB wanted to get rid of any or all of them, he wouldn't have had much trouble. They weren't the kind of people cops go looking for or parents mourn."

Portia's stomach rolled. "Thanks, you've been a great help."

"Maybe. You know these girls? Is that what this is really about?"

"No. Never heard of them. I can't tell you right now what started me on this. It's simply a suspicion I have."

"If you take it to the cops, let me know. I'd like to see how this ends."

"I will."

"Promise?"

"You bet."

***

Armed with the information Walt had provided, Portia researched the women's names, stopping only to grab some orange juice. To her surprise, Ty wasn't on the sofa any longer or anywhere else in the cottage. It was also well past lunch with Nick not having returned.

Worried, she hurried outside, stopping on her front porch. He, Ty, and other pack members stood near the damaged cottage, the gaping hole Ty had fallen through covered with a bright-blue tarp. With Nick in the lead, they trekked to Fran's house.

Portia ducked back inside to her computer, locating public utility records for Marie and Brooke. Marie had relocated to Fort Myers. The restaurant where she worked posted photos on their website, along with related articles profiling wait staff. The most recent one was from last month. Marie had escaped Kent's grip alive. Given her cheery smile, she also looked happy and safe.

The same for Brooke. She lived in Naples now, working for a pet care service. Photos showed her shampooing dogs and cats, the pictures and accompanying pieces also having recent dates.

Trish's trail never went beyond this area. The information on her stopped after Walt left for Georgia and before the pack settled in Moonlight, a previously abandoned location, the developer not having enough funds to renovate the bungalows. Even with the pack here now, this rural enclave wasn't on anyone's destination. Abandoned orange groves, along with Shelley Fields' small farm and orchard, protected the community from prying eyes and too many questions.

Her gut ached. She hoped she was wrong about this, that Trish was alive, working somewhere, and had possibly hooked up with a nice guy.

Portia tried every way possible to find something on the young woman. Police records, utility searches, and people locators turned up zip.

Maybe Trish had gotten married and changed her last name. That would explain a lot. Portia keyed hurriedly, Googling how to search a woman's married name to tie in with her maiden one, or vice versa. Whatever worked.

"You forgot about me."

She flinched and turned to Nick. Behind him, thin sun poured through the window, its angle proving how late it was.

"Bad girl." He eased her computer aside. "You know what that means, don't you?"

He'd washed and changed into fresh jeans, chest and feet bare, his scent musky-clean, hair dangling over his forehead, sin filling his eyes.

Hard lust edged out her worries, her need for him too great to deny. "I've never been this bad before. Tell me what it means."

"Screw that. I intend to show you. Get up and take off your shorts." He padded back. "Now."

Her cutoffs hit the floor, the tap sounding too loud, the same as her walloping heart. She reached up to unhook her bra.

"Leave it on. Bend over the table, legs spread, ass high."

Her partial nudity was more arousing than she

could have believed, her pussy congesting with heat. After assuming the position, she looked over.

"Face front. No moving or speaking until I'm through with you."

She couldn't wait for him to do her good.

He roamed from side to side, his feet slapping the floor. Other than that, everything went strangely quiet, him studying her nudity. She flushed at how she must look, both openings available for his use, her soft folds already plump and wet, inviting him inside.

That wasn't his goal, was it? At least not yet. She'd been bad, forgetting about him, neglecting his needs—a good reason for punishment. Not the cruel or hurtful kind. A game they could both play, with him as her master, she his willing slave.

He grasped her hip, his touch firm.

Her breath caught.

"Ass higher. Show me you want this."

More than she would have guessed. She lifted her buttocks as much as possible, begging for his discipline.

He paddled her, each smack quick, crack upon

crack ringing through the room. The sting surprised, though not as much as the blessed heat that followed. When he stopped, she pushed into him, wanting more.

A rasp sounded, the noise a zipper makes when lowered. His jeans rustled next, whooshing to the floor then sliding across the linoleum. He entered her without foreplay, swift, sure, and deep, their bodies tapping, him grunting with brazen disregard, his cock brutally thick and beyond hard, claiming her.

She surrendered fully, lost in an erotic haze. A man taking a woman who wanted nothing more than him mounting, filling, using her for both their pleasure.

Nick pumped tirelessly. He stroked and teased her nub.

Portia's skin burned, perspiration coating her. She tightened her sheath around his pounding rod, intensifying the resistance.

Growling, he thrust faster, harder, forcing her to the edge and beyond. She shattered, her pussy so turgid with lust it embraced his rod firmly. He came on a wild cry, jerking her toward him, not stopping.

At last, exhaustion slowed him down, his gasps ragged, her sheath pulsing rhythmically around his shaft. Sated, she pillowed her hands beneath her cheek, ready to nap.

Nick pulled her up, his arm snaking around her waist, free hand holding hers to her chest. Her head lolled back, too heavy to lift. He pushed his foot against hers, directing Portia to spread her legs. Once she had, he kept his feet inside of hers. Odd, but nice. "Careful, we might fall."

"Never." He stroked her nub.

Incomparable feelings flared. She writhed, unable to bear the staggering delight or close her legs to keep him from touching her there. This was too much too soon, her clit super sensitive. "Hold it-hold it-hold it. Give me a sec."

He pressed his mouth to her ear, his bristly cheek scraping hers. "You really want that?"

He could turn her inside out, upside-down and she'd still crave more. She was hopeless. "Do your worst. I can take anything."

"Let's see." He stroked her slowly, maddeningly, veering from her clit to circle the surrounding area, giving her a moment's peace that she didn't want. The precious tension and ache faded. Before they disappeared completely, he returned to her nub, his touch firm and fast.

She stiffened. He slowed down. No, no, no. She didn't want him to stop. Wiggling, she tried to rub her clit against his fingers. He brushed her thigh instead. She released her weight into him, yielding to whatever he willed.

He played with her sex as a man would with a prized possession, his touch careful and searching yet sure. Utterly fantastic. Jubilant, Portia delivered everything she was or would ever be to him. Her pleasure in his hands.

Nick drew out the act, fuzzing her mind, breaking down whatever barriers remained. She came on a shudder, rather than a loud cry, fully spent, heat, elation, and contentment gliding through her.

With surprising grace, he freed his cock from her channel and turned Portia to face him, gathering her into his arms. "Good?"

He'd left her no strength to hug him, her face pressed against his chest. "Do you really have to ask?"

He chuckled. "You like these types of games? Spanking and stuff?"

"Only with you."

"We'll have to do this again." He stifled a yawn. "I looked for you all afternoon, thinking you'd bring lunch or would want me to slap together a sandwich for you. Ty said you were talking to someone on the phone. None of my business I know, but he said you sounded upset. Are you all right?"

Her apprehension returned full blast. So much for great sex making her problems fade away permanently. "We can talk about it later. Why don't you take a nap while I fix dinner?"

He captured her wrist and brought her back. "I will when you give me an answer. Please. Are you all right?"

She couldn't lie to him. "I've found something that might tie into the accidents here."

His sleepy expression grew quickly alert. "What?"

"I think Kent killed his last girlfriend and buried her in the forest surrounding Moonlight."

Nick dropped into the chair, settling Portia on his lap. "Are you serious? You can't be. Admittedly, Kent's an A-hole, but a murderer, too?"

"I'm not saying he's a wild-eyed serial killer like you see on TV. But he is a control freak and abusive to women. From what Walt told me—"

"Hold it. Walt, his former partner? You called him?"

"I had to do something, the so-called accidents and stench is driving me nuts."

This was crazy. "What stench?"

"From Trish Quinn's body. What I've smelled for weeks that you haven't. Why not?"

"Baby." He cupped her face. "No one here has smelled anything, especially a decomposing body. Trust me. If they had, I would have heard about it. Are you saying this Trish disappeared recently and that he came onto pack grounds and buried her here?"

She pushed his hands away. "No, he did that before you guys moved to Moonlight because no one was here then. This area was abandoned, the perfect place to hide a corpse."

"If that's so, why didn't you notice the odor when you first got here? Even cadaver dogs can spot human decomposition up to thirty years after it's happened. I'm sure as shifters, we can as well, maybe better. How is it possible that none of us have, only you? And only now?"

"I don't know why it's taken me this long to notice or why I'm the only one who can smell it. Could be I was so upset about my parents, my senses were whacked out, I was depressed and not firing on all cylinders until I had some hope that you and I would hook up. Maybe I'm the only one who smells what's happened because I'm not from the same pack as you guys. Difference in DNA or something that maybe matches hers...Trish. It's also possible she's reaching out to me beyond the grave."

"Like a ghost? Portia, really—"

"Really, what? We're shifters. Is that any more reasonable in the so-called normal world than the dead contacting me? Could be Trish tried with you guys, but you weren't tuned in because of all the problems you'd encountered before coming here, and I'm simply more receptive, like Kevin Bacon in that old movie Stir of Echoes."

"I never saw it."

She blew out a sigh. "All right, then, think of me being like Riesa."

Riesa Marlowe was a human and a psychic who'd mated with Derek. "Now you're saying you have extrasensory abilities?"

"Why not? Trish's murder might have brought out a talent I didn't know I had, one that was dormant until I came here. That day you thought I didn't like your aftershave, I had just caught the odor again. Sickly sweet, like death. And don't tell me I don't know what that's like. I had to identify my parents after the accident. What I encountered in the morgue was the same odor as what's here. A stink I'll never forget."

Him either. He'd experienced it with his parents, pack members, and Bree, but never in Moonlight. "I've been around death a lot."

Her expression changed. She lowered her face. "I'm sorry. I didn't mean to bring up anything bad."

"You haven't. I'm simply saying I, and all the others here, should be able to recognize it, too."

"Not if you've encountered death so much. It might be like background noise to you now. It's there, but you don't sense it any longer, like odors in your house that you don't notice, but visitors will."

He supposed anything was possible, but that? "Are you certain Trish isn't hanging around somewhere? Maybe she moved."

"When Kent broke up with her, all records stopped, there's zip activity. I've been hoping she got married and changed her last name. That's what I was researching when you came in. Truthfully, I don't think she ever left the area."

"And that's why he's been screwing with us? Causing accidents?"

"I'm not saying it's smart, but my guess is he's getting increasingly desperate. Each day that passes is another one that could bring us closer to finding the grave. We're shifters. We run through the forest on a regular basis, crisscrossing all the territory, not one set path. He knows that and may figure luck isn't always going to be with him. If he causes enough grief and the pack takes off, his secret's already way safer, right? There's a lot of heavily vegetated land around here, but not many humans who are going to traipse through it. Not even hunters. Even with the country road passing through town, we're off the beaten path. I'm certain when he chose this spot to dump her he never dreamed shifters would settle here. This is probably his worse freaking nightmare come true. We can sense things humans can't and expose him. And unlike stray dogs that might accidentally sniff out a corpse, we can go to the authorities."

"Jesse and Charlie." They were Palmetto County Sheriff's detectives. Humans who were married to refugee shifters. Jesse's wife, Alexa, had arranged for the pack to move here. "You're going to tell those guys about this?"

"Not yet. I need more evidence. I don't want them blowing me off or causing anyone here to think I'm nuts, like Derek and Rand. Or the others to want me gone. That is, any more than they already do."

"Screw Fran and Olive. This is your home. How do you plan to get more evidence?" He cupped her chin. "Please don't tell me you're going to speak to Kent."

"Of course not. I'm not dumb. I want to search for Trish's body. Once I find her, I'll call the cops."

"You'll do that. Not us?"

She searched his face. "You want to help?"

Nick wanted this to go away, gorge on her fabulous meals, watch TV, screw like crazy, then fall asleep and do it all over again. Her suspicions were too surreal to take seriously. Yet, there were the weird accidents, the odor she smelled, and Kent showing up in the forest that one night. An odd occurrence at the time, though somewhat logical now. Nick had read how murderers often returned to crime scenes, either to relive their glory in killing someone or to make certain no one had found them out. "How do you think she died?"

"You believe me?"

Unfortunately. "It's too strange not to make sense once you put the pieces together. Do you think he planned to kill her?"

"Either that or he got in a rage because she was breaking free like Brooke and Marie had. They were his other long-term girlfriends. They're fine, by the way. With Trish, he might have simply lost it, struck out, and had to hide his crime."

"We can't search for her while it's light. The others

will wonder what we're doing."

"Then we'll wait until everyone's asleep and check as much area as we can."

This got crazier by the minute. "Should I bring a shovel?"

"Yeah."

***

Portia didn't want to be right. If she were, nothing would be good again until Trish went home...wherever that may be and whether anyone cared about her or not. She might end up in a potter's field, but at least she'd have a proper burial.

The cottages were dark, shifters quiet, night creatures chirping, buzzing, scurrying about. A half-moon cast the world in gray-and-black relief, no longer spellbinding, as the evening when she and Nick had mated for life.

He followed her into the woods, a beta position he didn't much like, having argued vigorously that he'd lead the way, assume all the risks, and take the proverbial bullet for her if he had to. Although they both had phenomenal wolf eyesight in the dark, her ability to smell this particular death had his beat hands down.

She lifted her face into the mucky breeze, perspiration rolling down her throat and between her breasts. Never had she been as hot, partly from the brutal temperature, mainly because of anxiety.

He edged close. "Smell anything?"

"Not yet." She'd whispered as he had.

"There's a place we should try first."

"Where?"

"Not too far from here. A while back, Kent was there in wolf form."

"Doing what?"

"Trying to avoid me. Come on." Nick took her hand and the lead. She hoped he wasn't doing this so he could run things.

With her chin lifted and neck craned, she sniffed. Nothing. After they'd walked quite a distance, she stopped. "How much farther? Even if it's five miles away, I should be able to start smelling it here if I caught it from way back there."

"How can you know for sure? The body's probably

bones by now except for some tissue and hair that might not give off scent like regular decay. Give it a chance. If you don't smell anything when we get there, we'll turn around."

Leaves crunched beneath their work boots, branches and saw palmettos lashed their legs. Bugs landed on her arms. Shivering, she brushed them off.

He squeezed her fingers. "Anything yet?"

"No."

Nick finally stopped and gestured to a thick stand, its contours a black mass in the dark. "That's where Kent was hiding."

Portia circled the area, sniffing, catching rabbit scent and bird droppings. No corpse. No Kent either. "Are you sure this is the right spot? He didn't leave any markings."

"I'm certain this is where he was. He surprised me so much, it's not something I'd forget." Nick lifted his face, testing the area, his frown deepening.

"You don't smell him either, do you?"

"No, but that doesn't mean anything. It's rained since then, probably washing his scent away."

"Do you think he was following you that night?"

"I don't know. Why? To make sure I didn't stumble across a grave?"

"You don't have to make it sound so preposterous."

"I'm not. I'm just asking."

"I don't know, then. Let's go back. I have a feeling she's closer to the community."

On the return trip, they took baby steps, checking everything out more than a few times, finally going in freaking circles. No matter how hard Portia tried, she couldn't catch the damn scent again. She slumped. "Maybe it's because it's dark. Every other time I've smelled it, it was during daylight."

Nick rubbed her arm. "Do you really think that would have anything to do with it?"

"I don't know. I've smelled all kinds of crappy stuff tonight, but not that...her. What if I can't find her and she stays out here forever?"

"Aw, baby." He hugged her gently. "That wouldn't be your fault. Maybe you detected an animal and it's gone now because predators picked it clean."

"Over several weeks?"

He rested his chin on her shoulder. "I'm really

trying to make sense of this."

He was far more patient than most men would have been. "Forgive me for dragging you out here. I should have let you sleep and done this alone."

"Never." He held her tightly against him. "We'll keep checking until dawn if you want."

She was too tired and sweaty, wanting a cold shower, clean sheets, and him next to her in bed. "Let's call it a night."

Several yards from the forest edge, she stopped, the stench overwhelming her. "Aw God. Here." She pointed down.

"We passed this on our way out. You didn't smell anything then."

"I do now. Give me the shovel."

Nick held it out of reach. "I'll dig." He scanned the forest floor in every direction. "Nothing's been disturbed here for a long time."

"It—she has to be close."

He checked the ground with Portia close behind. No matter where they stepped, the dirt was hard, packed tight, roots and vines peeking through, showing old growth. She kicked leaves aside, expecting to find a shallow grave. Those areas beneath the forest debris were untouched.

"Dammit, this doesn't make sense. I was so sure—"

Nick clamped his hand over her mouth, yanked her to her knees behind a bush, and inclined his head.

A large, gray wolf darted between Ty's cottage and Fran's, a pail hanging from its mouth, teeth clamped on the handle like something in a humorous commercial or Disney flick. It trotted across the next yard and jumped through the open window of an empty cottage Nick hadn't finished painting. Roofing repairs had interrupted him.

Portia tugged his hand away and pressed her lips to his ear. "Kent?"

He nodded.

She tested the air but didn't catch the man's scent. "Do you smell him?"

Nick sniffed. "No."

"How is that possible? We're downwind of him. I caught his scent in his store when he was in human form."

"Maybe his DNA is different from other shifters, like yours is with that odor only you detect. Could be he can turn his scent off and on at will to meet his purposes, keep everyone off guard."

"What do you think is in the pail?"

"Nothing good, that's for sure."

Portia pulled Nick down. "You can't confront him before he actually does something. He'll give you no end of excuses, and then he'll be far more careful. We'll never catch him."

"That may be. But what if he's planning to burn the cottage down, hoping the others go up in flames too, all of us dying?"

Crap. "If you're going after him, so am I."

"No."

"Fine. I'll go alone."

"No!"

She'd already pulled off most of her clothes. Swearing, he stripped. They shifted faster than usual and stayed upwind to keep Kent from sensing their approach, their movements painfully slow, the journey seemingly endless. Creeping from bush to bush, they hid behind each and waited to see if he'd come out. Nick finally dashed to the porch with her in close pursuit. Using his muzzle, he nudged the door open enough for them to slip through.

The front room was empty, as were the kitchen, bath, and bedroom. Kent was already outside, bounding across the backyard, disappearing into the forest.

Portia shifted to human form, as did Nick. There was no furniture in here for Kent to have messed with, just paint cans, brushes, tools. "Do you think he screwed with the paint? Put poison in there so the fumes would make us sick? No, don't check."

He pulled her hand off his. "He didn't open any of these. The dried stuff on the edges is still intact."

They padded from room to room. In the kitchen, Nick wrinkled his nose and opened the cabinet beneath the sink.

"Whoa." She held her breath. "What is that?"

"Primer, turpentine, paint, and thinner. These rags are soaked with it."

"They're not yours, right?"

"Hell no. Leaving this pile here would be nuts. When the cottage gets really hot, around midday or so, the fumes would ignite."

"Spontaneous combustion?"

"Yep. Prick." Nick looked up. "It's not that I didn't believe you before, but I certainly do now. Trish is out there somewhere. You and I are going to find her. We're going to nail the bastard."

Chapter Seven

Portia agreed with Nick that they should continue their search the following evening after everyone else was asleep.

When they were ready to return to the forest, she stopped him before leaving her cottage. "We should have told Ty what we're doing. Our suspicions."

"Why?"

"Kent. He's sure to come by to see what happened with those rags he planted."

"He could have driven past here during the day to check things out without us noticing. Even if he hadn't wanted to risk that, a fire would have been on the news. Since there wasn't a blaze, he must know by now that nothing happened."

"Which will bring him back here to do something

else. I doubt he's going to give up. We can't search for Trish and keep watch for him at the same time, especially since it appears he can hide his scent whenever he wants."

Nick woke Ty, explaining the situation.

The poor guy looked slightly comical with his prominent freckles, red hair sticking in every direction, and bewildered expression. "Shouldn't we tell Derek and Rand about this?"

"God, no." Portia sounded unglued but couldn't help it, since she was. "We'd like to keep this quiet until we have evidence to nail Kent."

Ty made a face. "What about the rags he left in the cottage? He'd have a hard time explaining why he'd do that."

"My guess is he'd simply claim it never happened. That Nick and I imagined the whole thing. It's not like we have him on video planting the stuff, which we couldn't use anyway given he'd shifted. What do we tell the authorities—those past Charlie and Jesse? That Kent has a trained wolf to do this stuff for him? I don't think so. When it comes to the human justice system or the rest of the world in general, we're pretty much screwed as shifters, and I'm sure he knows it."

"Well yeah, but how long will your search take? There's a lot of land out there. You could be at this for weeks or months."

"Just this one night, promise."

Nick looked surprised. "You're sure? If we don't find anything this evening, we tell the others what happened?"

Portia didn't see another choice. Despite her worry the pack would consider her delusional or a problem they didn't want around, she couldn't risk their safety. "Yeah."

Ty scratched his chest. "Go on. I'll keep an eye on things. But for shit's sake, be careful."

Nick squeezed the guy's shoulder. "Yes, Mom."

After the guys pretended to box and ended with a brotherly hug, Nick followed her to the porch, shovel in hand. "Where to first?"

Portia pulled out the map she'd made and kept her voice to a whisper. "I've drawn the spots where I've caught the odor. I'd like to start here." She pointed to a large red X on the paper, moonlight illuminating the sheet. "It's in the center of those places. From there, we can work our way outward, rather than searching blindly as we have been."

Ty slipped past them in wolf form and shot to the vegetation. Hidden within the brush, he sank to the ground, facing the community, alert for danger.

Nick took her hand. "Are you detecting the odor now, even a trace?"

"Not yet."

"Let's get started."

The area was huge, taking quite a while for them to trudge to its center. Panting, they searched the ground, kicking leaves and other debris aside. Nick wedged his shovel beneath a rotted log and hefted it a foot above the ground. Creepy crawlies scattered from their hiding places, many running over her work boots.

Portia suppressed a shiver and hunkered down for a better look.

"See or smell anything?"

"No."

They tossed aside rocks and moved limbs. Nick pounded the shovel tip into the ground, testing for soil that might have been disturbed at one time. Everything proved too solid, untouched by man.

She turned a slow circle, not knowing what to do next. "Come on, Trish, help us. Where. Are. You?"

The odor hit with such force, the corpse might have been hugging Portia. She staggered back.

Nick rushed over. "What?"

She wasn't certain how to answer. There should have been an obvious grave here, except there wasn't. It didn't make sense...then unexpectedly, it did. "We're on a blood trail." Those visible traces would have faded long ago, though not the smell. "That's what I've detected all along."

"Leading where? Why haven't we found the burial site?"

"Because it's everywhere." She flung out her arms. "Kent didn't dump her in one spot. He scattered her."

Even in the moonlight, Nick's color faded. "She's dismembered?"

"Or he tore her apart while he was in wolf form then buried or dumped her here."

"If he dumped her, there won't be anything left to recover. Animals would have taken care of that long ago."

"Except for large bones and the skull. Those he would have had to bury or risk detection. Oh, God."

"What?"

The stench was stronger than it had ever been. She wanted to believe Trish was proving the theory correct, guiding them to her remains. "We need to go over there."

Portia pointed and followed the odor. It faded slightly. She swerved to the left, picking it up again, and broke into a run.

Nick called from behind, "Watch out for the log!"

She lurched to a stop, a breath away from falling over the thing. "Something's here."

The scent practically smothered her. She fell to her knees and shoved the trunk.

"Hold on." Nick pulled her back. "I'll get it."

Using the shovel, he heaved the log to the side. It crashed against the ground, breaking into several pieces, sending dust and leaves flying. Insects swarmed in the shallow spot where it had laid, the ground dank and gooey. Portia was too riveted to care. In the drab light, something whitish poked through the muck.

They dug with their hands, unearthing a large bone. She sat on her heels. "That's a femur, right?"

"Looks to be."

"Human? An adult?"

"I'm no doctor, but I'd say yes."

"Look." She fingered the top, teeth marks in the bone, parts broken away. "A wolf could do that."

"He must have torn her apart, just as you said."

"I didn't want to be right." She bowed her head, fighting tears.

Nick pulled her into him then loosened his hold immediately. "Fuck, my hands are muddy. Give me a sec to wipe them off before I make you too dirty."

"I don't care." She embraced him.

They hung onto each other. He stroked her back. "Is the odor still around?"

"Stronger than ever. There's more we have to find." The stench no longer made her ill. It smelled of justice and peace. Although Trish would always remain a stranger, Portia sensed a bond between them unlike anything she'd known.

Nick released her. "Where to now?"

She looked over, the odor drawing her. "To the left. Wait. What about the bone? We can't rebury it. The cops would know someone screwed around with this place, contaminating evidence."

"If we leave the bone here, uncovered, an animal will probably take off with it before we can bring anyone back."

"We'll have to take it with us. Whatever we find next, we better leave things as they are, as much as we can."

"Agreed."

She followed the invisible blood trail, took a detour to the right, and stopped.

Nick was beside her immediately, shovel in one hand, thighbone in his other. "Where?"

She pointed. Like the femur, a whitish object gleamed dully beneath bushes, barely visible in the scant moonlight. Someone would have had to look hard and long to have caught it.

Nick put down the shovel and bone.

On their knees, they eased aside branches, careful not to disturb the scene any more than necessary. Mud had partially buried the skull, its right side exposed, revealing an empty eye socket, nasal cavity, and upper teeth. Hair had tangled in the lower branches, the tresses long and blonde like Trish's in her DMV photo.

The odor subsided then blasted back, thick and suffocating. Leaves rustled. Twigs snapped.

Portia looked over. Kent swung the shovel.

Nick shoved her away. The blade clipped his shoulder, blood pouring from the wound. She screamed. Backing away, Kent swung the shovel wildly. While dodging the blows, Nick shifted.

Portia changed as quickly. Canines bared, she approached from the opposite side, she and Nick surrounding Kent. He jabbed the shovel at Nick then suddenly hurled the thing at her. She leaped, the flat end smacking her croup. White-hot pain seared through her. She tumbled to the ground.

Nick howled, an unearthly sound fueled by rage. He jumped.

Kent spun away, shifting quickly, and bounded into the brush.

Nick followed a few yards then stopped and glanced back at her. She struggled to her paws and ran to him. Shoulder to shoulder they tore through the forest, predators and guardians, determined to protect and kill.

They may as well have been following a ghost. Kent's gray fur matched the moonlight drizzling down. He had no damn smell due to a genetic mutation or from something he'd done to himself chemically.

If he got away....

The stench returned, beckoning, guiding. Portia ran toward it, Nick following her. They shot past saw palmettos and leaped over bushes. Gray flashed in the distance. Not moonlight.

Portia ran as never before, Nick by her side. He bolted ahead and nipped Kent's tail. The wolf yelped and thrashed. Breaking free, he sped away.

No!

***

Blood drenched Nick's shoulder, agony shooting through him with each move he made. Ignoring the pain, he pushed harder, ran swifter, and sunk his teeth into the SOB's tail.

Kent jerked back and howled, but still fought to get free.

Nick bit into the tail, not enough to sever, but to deny escape. He swung Kent to the right and left as he would a rag doll or a carcass. Kent's paws slammed into a large rock, his head knocked against a trunk. He still twisted and struggled, refusing to give up.

Portia bit his shoulder, tearing away the flesh.

Tortured sounds poured from him. He flailed his paws and snapped his teeth at her.

Nick clamped his jaws on the bastard's throat, severing his jugular and carotid arteries. Kent stiffened then shuddered, his limbs twitching in death throes.

After spitting out the blood, Nick shifted as Portia had and crawled to her. "Are you all right?"

She wiped blood from her mouth, spitting it away as he had. "Yeah."

"Let me see your hip where he hit you."

"It's okay. Your shoulder." She touched the wound.

Already, the flow had stopped, his muscles bruised, no bones broken. "Did he bite you anywhere?"

"No. You?"

Nick shook his head. "If he had, I'd seriously consider getting rabies shots."

She laughed then covered her face and cried.

"Hey, it's over." His hands hovered, him not knowing where to touch her, possibly upsetting her more. "Nothing to be sad about. I killed him. You didn't."

"Screw him. You could have died." She grabbed his biceps and shook him hard. "Why do you keep taking risks?"

"To protect you."

"To hell with that. I want you safe."

"I'm fine. Nothing you say is going to change my mind about protecting you, got it?"

She growled and slammed her fist into her thigh.

"I'll do my best. There's something I have to ask you."

"The answer is no. If you insist on being macho man and chancing death, I will, too, all right?"

"That's not what I was getting at. And no, it's not okay. But back to my question—how did you know where to find him without his scent?"

"Trish told me."

Nick warned himself not to act surprised. "She's speaking to you now?"

Portia laughed, somewhat hysterically. "I'm not hearing voices. The odor returned. I simply followed it to him. Who else but Trish could have sent it?"

No one that Nick knew of.

In death, Kent had reverted to human form, the gaping wound in his throat nearly decapitating him. Although Nick's savagery surprised him, he didn't regret what he'd done to save Portia and avenge Trish. He simply wished the situation hadn't gone this far. "I'm glad she helped you out. We'll have to leave him here while we go back and alert the others."

"As in Derek and Rand, or them and the cops?"

"We'll begin with the pack."

They started back, arms around each other's waists, needing the support. She limped from her bruised hip. He had trouble ignoring his gashed shoulder, which hurt like a son-of-a-bitch. Even holding onto the femur made his muscles tighten and ache. Once they'd pulled on their clothes, they dragged to the forest edge.

Portia inhaled sharply. Nick bit back an oath and strode to Ty, who'd shifted back to human form. On the ground, he held his head in his hands, and rocked.

Nick leaned down. "Did Kent hit you?"

"Someone fucking did. I was watching the cottages then bam, I woke up with the mother of all headaches."

"Let me see." Portia eased his hair aside. Ty winced. He had a huge bump on his skull, his hair matted with darkened blood.

Nick squeezed his shoulder. "You all right now, except for the pain?"

"No. I'm tired of this shit. I want things to return to the way they were before."

Portia patted his knee. "They will. Right, Nick?"

Ty looked from her to him. "What's that mean? You found something?"

"Kent. He's dead. I killed him." Nick pushed to his feet. "I'll get Derek and Rand."

***

Portia was beginning to hate Moonlight Diner. She could barely keep still as Nick explained the situation to the guys. Thankfully, they were the only pack members here, so far. When the rest were notified....

She didn't want to think about it.

After Nick explained everything, Derek pushed into his chair, balancing it on the back legs. "Why didn't you come to us before you involved yourself in this?"

"Oh hey, wait." She leaned across the table to Derek. "It's not Nick's fault. It's mine."

"The hell it is." He pulled her back. "Let me handle this."

"Why should you have to? You would never have gotten involved if it hadn't been for me. I should have kept my big mouth shut."

"If you had, Kent could have burned the community down and killed all of us. I'm glad you spoke up."

"I could have battled him on my own. I should

have. Can you ever forgive me?"

"Guys." Derek folded his hands behind his head. "You both should have come to Rand and me. We have a dead body in the forest, remember?"

"Totally my fault." Portia put out her wrists. "Slap the cuffs on me. I'm guilty."

Nick pushed her hands down. "It was self-defense. Are you going to tell Jesse and Charlie about this?"

Dead freaking silence.

Portia wasn't certain if that was good or bad. "You're not going to throw Nick out of the pack are you? For myself, that's fine."

"What?" Nick glared at her. "If you go, so do I."

"Neither of you has to leave." Derek settled his chair on four legs and looked at Portia. "As to Trish's scent leading you to Kent...do you really think you're psychic, or have paranormal abilities, or whatever you want to call it?"

"I don't know. If it happened once, I suppose it could happen again."

"You should get together with Riesa. Compare notes."

"I'll do that. Thanks."

"If you sense anything again, you come to us first. No playing Murder She Wrote in your spare time."

Nick slung his arm around her shoulders. "She was amazing, but she'll behave from now on. Won't you, baby." He shook her gently.

She elbowed him. "I'll try."

Hey, that's all she could promise.

With that settled, Derek called the meeting, explaining to the pack what had happened, including Portia's unexpected gift, and that he and Rand would handle matters. Wisely, no one pressed them on particulars. The less they knew.... However, Kent couldn't simply disappear from the planet with no one wondering why. He had a business.

Portia straightened in her chair, an idea forming that she couldn't wait to get to, as soon as this business was done.

"Okay, that's it." Derek pushed back his chair. "Meeting's over."

Fran stood. "Not so fast, I have something to say."

Nick groaned softly. Portia warned herself not to react to whatever nasty thing Fran said. Wasn't worth it. She and Nick were here for life and had to get along with the pack.

Fran faced her.

God, this was going to be bad. "Yeah?"

"I'm sorry. I misjudged you. I apologize." She approached and stuck out her hand. "Can we forget everything, start over, and shake on it?"

Portia hugged the older woman. "I'm sorry, too, for the mean things I said and that I didn't catch Kent sooner."

"You did an amazing job. May he rot in hell."

"I'm sure that's where he is."

Fran patted her back. "Welcome to Moonlight."

Forever.

Epilogue

Months later....

The summer day was ungodly hot and humid. Clouds smeared across the sky turning everything hazy white. Luckily, it wasn't raining or lightning. Portia didn't want even worse weather spoiling today.

After zipping her black sundress, she grabbed her black ballet flats. "Babe, you almost done?"

"I'm hurrying as fast as I can."

"The ceremony starts in a few minutes. If we don't leave soon, everyone's going to melt by the time we get there."

Nick padded from the bath to the closet, his cock swinging, butt cheeks bouncing.

So drool-worthy, she had to resist touching him.

Her poor self-control was the reason they were running late. His, too. Neither had wanted to leave their bed.

He pushed hangers aside. "Where's my good shirt?"

"To the right."

"You sure jeans will be okay for this?"

"They'll have to be. You don't have anything else." She brushed her hair. "Trish won't mind. What's important is the pack showing up."

They were holding a service for her today in Moonlight, laying her bones to rest here. Portia and Nick had searched for weeks, unable to find each one. The odor was finally gone, no longer helping them. Although Trish had moved on, Portia wanted a nice place for her earthly remains. Nick helped with cleaning the bones they had, arranging them carefully in a white enameled box lined with yellow satin— Trish's favorite color according to her old Facebook page. It wasn't the best funeral but would have to do. Even with Jesse and Charlie's help, only two relatives turned up. Trish's mother had died years ago from an overdose. Once her father learned he wouldn't be responsible for burial costs, he was disinterested in anything having to do with his child. He'd told Portia to do what she wanted with the remains. Not his problem.

Wasn't right. Everyone should have family, someone who worried about them.

The pack had become Trish's relations. She'd helped them stop Kent and would always be in their hearts.

Walt's, too. He'd sent a beautiful arrangement for today, yellow roses and baby's breath. Shortly after the meeting in Moonlight Diner, Portia had contacted him about Kent's passing.

He never asked how the man had died. Whatever Derek, Rand, Charlie, or Jesse had done about the matter, it never made the news. Given Kent's toxic personality, no one missed him either.

There was his business, though. She'd approached Walt about coming back to run things. Who better to see to the area's needs, especially since Kent had cheated him out of his share. Walt had returned a month ago and had everything running smoothly again, happier than he'd ever been.

"Done." Nick tossed his comb on the dresser. Strands of his midnight hair dangled over his forehead, others curled obediently on his neck and behind his ears.

Far too tamed and perfect. She liked his hair bed-mussed, cheeks bristly, his beautiful body buck-naked, his hard-on massive enough to make women swoon, telling them how lucky she was. She'd always be grateful for finding him, with him loving her in return. "You shouldn't have shaved."

"Now you tell me." He winked. "You look good enough to eat."

"For dessert, after the gathering at Fran's place. She and Olive are putting out a spread."

"Who would've thought."

No kidding. Olive and Fran were motherly now, adopting Portia and Nick as their "kids." The ladies were still intrusive, but meant well.

He held out his hand. "You ready for this?"

"Never. I wish we were going to Trish's wedding instead. But this will have to do."

"She'll never be without home or family again."

"Neither will we."

Smiling, he wrapped his arm around her shoulders and led her outside into the moist breeze.

About the Author

Tina is an Amazon and international bestselling novelist in erotic, paranormal, contemporary and historical romance. Booklist, Publisher's Weekly, Romantic Times and numerous online sites have praised her work.

Before penning romances, she worked at a major Hollywood production company in Story Direction.